A SHOT FROM THE DARK

Holmes placed the candle on the desk and was turning back to his work when the upper pane of one of our bay windows was shattered. There was a booming sound; the candle was abruptly halved, and there was a resounding thud in the far side of the room.

"Holmes, we are being fired upon!" I cried, dropping from the desk chair and making for the window on all fours.

"Calm yourself, old fellow," said the sleuth in a casual tone. To my consternation he made for the door to our chambers with no attempt at concealment. Retrieving the upper portion of the candle from the floor, he commented, "Remarkable piece of shooting. Had the marksman fired at a human target one of us would now be dead."

SHERLOCK HOLMES
AND
THE TREASURE TRAIN
FRANK THOMAS

PINNACLE BOOKS NEW YORK

This novel is a work of fiction. Names, characters, places, and incidents are either the product of the author's imagination or are used fictitiously. Any resemblance to actual events or places or persons, living or dead, is entirely coincidental.

SHERLOCK HOLMES AND THE TREASURE TRAIN

Copyright © 1985 by Frank Thomas

An original Pinnacle Books edition, published for the first time anywhere.

First printing/March 1985

ISBN: 0-523-42045-5
Can. ISBN: 0-523-43461-8

Printed in the United States of America

PINNACLE BOOKS, INC.
1430 Broadway
New York, New York 10018

9   8   7   6   5   4   3   2   1

Holed up at Charing Cross during the Blitz in London, Frank Thomas discovered a battered tin dispatch box crammed with papers. Here were Dr. Watson's records of unpublished cases by the world-famous detective, Sherlock Holmes. After years of legal battles, Frank Thomas has now brought to light SHERLOCK HOLMES AND THE TREASURE TRAIN, adapted from the memoirs of John H. Watson, M.D.

Contents

SHERLOCK HOLMES
AND
THE TREASURE TRAIN

Chapter 1

❧

The Refusal

WHEN MY FRIEND Sherlock Holmes and I were finally ushered into the conference room of the Birmingham and Northern Railroad, I must have shown surprise. The building that housed the great transportation company shared the yellow brick sameness of its neighbors in the Waterloo area. Its nerve center was, however, a far cry from early nineteenth-century architecture, being reminiscent of the great hall of an ancient feudal keep. Stucco walls soared better than two stories to a curved ceiling of stout timbers joined by cast-iron straps. The door to this impressive chamber was of carved oak. A massive fireplace into which I could have stepped without bending my head dominated one wall. Around it, flintlock muskets and swords of various ages hung vertically. In their midst, on a short staff, was a regimental banner, which I judged to be Russian, a captured memento of the Crimea. In front of the fireplace was a long trestle table flanked by benches. A large Jacobean armchair was positioned at each end. The oak gleamed of oil and the flickering light of burning logs threw

1

dancing shadows on the table and adjacent arti-
facts. Twin lighting fixtures hung from chain hoists
over each end of the table and provided the only
modern touch to a scene that provoked an immediate impression of solidity and grandeur.

Under different circumstances I might have been
prompted to pose questions regarding the many
obviously authentic mementos that were the warp
and woof of the room's character, as might Holmes,
as he had indulged in a flirtation with medieval
architecture at one time. However this was not to
be, for things took a different turn—and not one for
the better, I should add.

The whole affair had gotten off to a bad start,
beginning with the somewhat peremptory summons to the B & N building. At the time I had been
surprised when the master sleuth abandoned our
chambers at 221B Baker Street to come to the
headquarters of the rail empire, though its president, Alvidon Daniel Chasseur, was a potential
client of acknowledged solvency. Upon arrival at
the formerly select residential neighborhood, now
destroyed by the coming of the railways, we had
been allowed to cool our heels in a drafty outer
office while news of our arrival was relayed
through a chain of command. Holmes, accustomed
to being welcomed with red-carpet gratitude,
adopted an imperious attitude toward the entire
proceedings, which was not soothed by the manner
of Mr. Chasseur or his board of directors, for such is
what I judged the others seated at the table to be.

The rail tycoon, hunched in one of the armchairs,
waved us toward a free space on the bench at his
left while concluding some words with a grizzled
man on his immediate right. Facing him, at the
other end of the long table, was a fair and youngish
looking chap who had the grace to rise at our

arrival. His face was clean-shaven and rugged. I judged him to be in his early thirties, which made him the youngest man in the room.

Having concluded his comments to his nearest employee, Chasseur now deigned to devote his attention to Holmes.

As he brushed back an errant wisp of white hair, the tycoon fastened large, rather myopic eyes on Holmes in an abrupt manner, which I was sure had struck terror in friends and adversaries as well on numerous occasions. Holmes, his face impassive, returned the stare without a flicker of emotion. The financier never so much as favored me with a glance. I was part of the furniture, as were his associates around the table, though he did single one out at this point.

"Mr. Holmes, we wish to discuss the matter of the gold shipment stolen from the Birmingham and Northern's special flyer but a short time ago. It was our security chief, Richard Ledger, who brought your name to my attention."

A flick of a bony forefinger indicated the youngish man I had noted at the other end of the table. Chasseur paused as though expecting an expression of gratitude from Holmes and, when none was forthcoming, continued, his voice dry and rather grating.

"My first impulse was to enlist the aid of the world's foremost detective, Monsieur Alphonse Bertillon, since the French have some involvement in this matter. My second thought was one of our Scotland Yard inspectors, like Lestrade, who do involve themselves in problems other than their official activities on occasion."

Chasseur again paused to allow the fact to sink in that Sherlock Holmes was but a third choice foisted on him. I took the moment to bid an adieu to the matter of the B & N Railroad. This despite the fact that we had not been involved in a profitable case for some time. Neither the pursuit of the Golden Bird nor the adventure involving the Sacred Sword had resulted in a fee, while incurring considerable expense. However, Chasseur had effectively shunted my friend from the gold robbery and he might better have been occupied waving a red flag in a bullring in Toledo. Had we been in some earlier time, when men were prone to vent their spleen with violent action, I could easily picture Holmes tearing one of the swords from the wall and carving Chasseur up like a Christmas goose. Instead, he placidly viewed the aged financier. The silence became nerve-racking and those around the table stirred uneasily. Finally Chasseur had to give in to the mood of the moment and added to his comments, though in a slightly more conciliatory tone.

"Ledger has considerable faith in your ability, Mr. Holmes. He was formerly with the army of India and is the finest big game hunter in the world."

By this time, I was as nervous as a cat and denied, with effort, the impulse to cross my legs or make some movement that would relieve the tenseness that had crept, nay galloped, into the scene. To my relief, Holmes finally contributed to the conversation, and in an even tone of voice, which must have cost him dearly.

"It has been said that one should follow first impulses, and relative to that, I shall make some mention of matters which might prove helpful. Gratis, of course."

Unable to divine the direction of the wind, the financier was now gazing at Holmes with the first shadow of surprise infiltrating his large eyes.

"The esteemed Bertillon's forte is identification

based on his Bertillonage system. He is not an 'in the field' operative. Lestrade is no doubt already involved in your affair since he seems to have a way of getting assigned to the most newsworthy cases. If you consider additional Scotland Yard assistance, you might think of Hopkins or Gregson or Alec MacDonald, who gives evidence of becoming the best of the lot. I know of all their work, being a consulting detective."

"I am not familiar with that title," said Chasseur quickly.

"No surprise since I am the only one in the world. A consulting detective has his services solicited by other professionals when they arrive at dead ends. I have but recently solved a little matter for Francis leVillard, a compatriot of Bertillon. A matter, I might add, which the Sûreté Nationale was completely incapable of dealing with."

Chasseur made as though to comment, but Holmes was in full stride now and I relaxed, somewhat gleefully, anticipating the chips to fall from the tycoon's oak under the blows of Holmes's verbal ax.

"In dealings with whatever investigatory means you choose, I suggest accuracy in your reports."

Chasseur's eyes grew even larger with a combination of amazement and anger. "I am scrupulous in that regard," he said, and would have said more if given the chance.

"A statement made in haste, sir. But a moment ago you referred to Mr. Ledger as the finest big game hunter in the world. The gentleman would, I'm sure, agree that Colonel Sebastian Moran occupies that niche."

Ledger rapidly confirmed the sleuth's contention. "Moran, of course, is unique," he stated with a deferential nod of his head toward Holmes.

"Was," corrected the sleuth. "May I remind you that the infamous colonel sometime back abandoned big game for different prey. I was his target, which is why he now languishes behind bars, where I put him."

Holmes must have felt that this dramatic announcement was as good an exit line as any, for he rose to his feet and I hastened to match his movements. There was a humorous touch to the moment. The directors of the railroad and their president resembled a school of guppies, every man regarding us with a slack jaw.

"Now, gentlemen, my associate and I bid you good day."

Chasseur almost choked trying to find words. No fool, he knew what was happening but still didn't quite accept it.

"Mr. Holmes, do you expect me to believe that you are refusing to act on behalf of the B & N Railroad?"

"I expect nothing from you," stated my friend, making for the door. Suddenly Holmes came to a halt, and I almost stumbled on his heels. He fixed the financier with his steely glance and the strength of his commanding personality was a tangible thing in the great room.

"You are forced," he continued in a measured tone, "to accept the fact that I have no intention of investigating the gold robbery for you."

As the sleuth opened the oak door for our departure, leaving the group of astonished men in his wake, Chasseur rallied with a parting shot.

"A moment, sir," he called. I turned, as did my friend, and noted that the rail magnate was now standing, a faint smile playing around the corners of his mouth. Subconsciously, I interpreted it as a gesture of defeat.

"I pride myself on accuracy, Mr. Holmes. If Ledger here does not fill the bill and Moran is incarcerated, then who is the leading big game hunter?"

Holmes replied in a lighter tone. "I care not a fig for who is the finest heavy game shot or most wily *shikari* our eastern empire has produced, for man is the most dangerous game. If you ask me who is the greatest man hunter, the answer is simple. Sherlock Holmes of Baker Street."

As he strode from the room and I hastened after him, my concern regarding our financial state fled like the dreams of yesteryears. Never could I recall an interview that came to such a gratifying conclusion. In the field of accomplishment, the entire incident contributed not one whit of good, but it had been so delightfully satisfying to that childish ego that lurks in all of us. If the boost to my morale proved costly, so be it. Such are the feelings of one living in reflected glory. A rebuff to Holmes was a slight to me, for I shared in his triumphs and defeats.

As we strode from the Birmingham and Northern building and into the brilliantly gas-lit station-bar nearby for a libation, I was ready to wager five against one that the pompous Alvidon Chasseur would not try and play fast and loose with the likes of Sherlock Holmes again.

Chapter 2

❧

An
Interesting Puzzle
in Rural Surroundings

AFTER HIS JOUST with the world of high finance, Holmes was not inclined to hail a hansom and return to Baker Street. Instead, the underground took us as far as Aldersgate. From there we walked to a vegetarian restaurant close-by Saxe-Coburg Square, where we enjoyed a light lunch. By now I realized what he had in mind and was not surprised when we then made for St. James's Hall. Sure enough, there was a Sarasate concert and I spent the greater part of the afternoon wrapped in the subtle rhythms of the great Spanish musician.

It was still daylight when we descended from the hansom that had brought us back to Baker Street. I had my latch key ready but was not allowed to use it for the front door burst open at our approach, revealing Billy. The page boy had evidently been watching for our arrival from within. His face mirrored concern as he extended a telegram toward the great detective.

"Mr. 'Olmes—I'm that put out."

"About a telegram, Billy? We receive lots of

those, goodness knows." Holmes's voice was soothing.

And send a few as well, I thought.

"But, sir, I don't know when this 'ere missive came," responded Billy, closing the outer door behind us. "Mrs. 'Udson didn't 'ear the bell, bein' in back cleanin' the 'ole bleeding arfternoon and I was not on ta premises."

Billy fancied words like *missive* and *premises*, which he had acquired via his close contact with Holmes.

Our concerned page boy now picked up a bulky package from the hall table.

"Then, just 'afore you come, this package arrived. The bloke wot brought it said it 'ad been sent by train from Shaw wiv instructions to be delivered by special messenger on arrival."

"Perhaps the telegram will explain the package," said Holmes, mounting the stairs. "Best come up with us, Billy, as fast action may be called for."

Within our sitting room, Holmes opened the telegram, which his eyes devoured rapidly.

"No mystery here," he said. "Billy, have a hansom downstairs in fifteen minutes. Then hustle over to the cable office and send a message to Constable Bennett, Police Station, Shaw. 'Leaving five-thirty from Paddington. Holmes.'" The detective looked at Billy keenly. "You can remember that, I'm sure."

Billy tapped his head with a forefinger. "Word fer word, Mr. 'Olmes. I'm on me way."

Billy took what he called "the detectin' business" seriously.

As the door closed behind our page boy, Holmes posed a question.

"Can you throw some things in a bag quickly,

Watson? I have had previous dealings with one
John Bennett, who is the constable in Shaw. It is a
little country town in Herefordshire. Bennett is
experiencing difficulties relative to the Trelawney
matter and requests assistance."

I needed no urging. My army experience with the
Northumberland Fusiliers had made me a prompt
traveler and Holmes was certainly used to what
seagoers call "the pierhead jump." It was but a
short time later that we were aboard the five-thirty
at Paddington. Holmes, with his long gray traveling cloak and cloth cap, disposed of a small valise
and placed the bulky package, which had just made
the same trip in reverse, alongside him on the seat.
I put a larger bag in the luggage rack, and we
settled down for our trip to Herefordshire. Soon we
were traveling westward at fifty miles an hour and
far removed from familiar surroundings.

"Perhaps you will explain the Trelawney matter," I suggested, "as well as that package evidently
sent to us in some haste."

"Fortunately, I have a grip on the essential facts
of the Trelawney case," replied Holmes. "This
parcel contains the recent papers from the area,
which we can study on the way down. The London
press made very brief reference to the affair. I can
tell you that Ezariah Trelawney, a banker by trade,
was murdered while alone in his house in Shaw.
The cause of death was a severe blow by a blunt
weapon on the back of his head. As I understand it,
an adopted son, Charles Trelawney, is in custody
now on suspicion of murder. Bennett's telegram
made reference to the Silver Blaze affair but did
not explain the connection. Since we are fortunate
in having this carriage to ourselves, I suggest we go
through these country journals and see what addi-

tional facts we can uncover. In the bucolic surroundings of Herefordshire, a murder is bound to capture a major portion of the newsprint."

I was glad to bury myself in the contents of the package sent by Constable Bennett for our perusal on the lengthy trip. Naturally, I searched for some unusual fact that might excite an idea in Holmes's mind. My friend read at intervals, interrupted by pauses for reflection, as though arranging the facts. We were long past Reading when I broke the silence.

"Here's something that might be of interest, Holmes. A complete coverage of Charles Trelawney's testimony before the coroner's court of inquiry."

"I've already read another account, but let us see what your paper has to offer."

As Holmes pored over the newspaper I handed him, it was pleasant to lean back for a moment to relax. Darkness had long since fallen. The train was steaming through the Stroud Valley and approaching the Severn River when my head jerked upward with a start and I realized that I'd dozed off. Holmes was gazing out the window at the passing darkness. There was little to see outside the speeding train and what there was Holmes was not conscious of. His eyes had that deep, introspective look that signified that his mercurial brain was flitting over pieces of the puzzle and fitting them into a mosaic of the mind.

Sensing my awakening, the master sleuth turned toward me with a slow smile. "Some sleep may prove of future benefit," he said. "We could very well have busy times ahead of us."

I indicated the newspapers scattered around the compartment. "Has anything suggested itself to you?"

"At the moment I'm suffering from a plethora of surmise, conjecture, and hypothesis. Let us see what we have been able to discover up to this time."

Holmes leaned back in his seat, gazing at the ceiling, and his words wandered over the facts at our disposal.

"Ezariah Trelawney was a widower who lived with his adopted son, Charles. There had been indications of a recent strain in their relations, a point which the coroner's inquest did not pursue to any appreciable depth. It was the banker's habit to sit before the fire in his study of an evening, reading the works of Thackeray. Death was definitely established as occurring between the hours of eight and ten. Constable Bennett evidently was able to secure a forensic medicine expert promptly. The body was discovered at eleven in the evening by Charles Trelawney, who stated that he had just returned from Hereford, where he had been on business. According to his testimony, his adopted father was seated in his customary chair, his head slumped forward from the fatal blow. The windows of the room were closed. The door leading into the room was closed but not locked. Now, Charles Trelawney contends that he had just arrived on the ten forty-five from Hereford. However, in countertestimony, the stationmaster at Shaw states that he definitely saw him arrive previously on the six o'clock special. It was the testimony of the stationmaster and some other evidence that resulted in Charles Trelawney's receiving a verdict of suspicion of murder at the inquest. Pending further investigation, the case is to go before the magistrates in Hereford."

"What other evidence do you refer to, Holmes?"

"Possibly, the papers you read stated there were two occupants in the Trelawney household. The cook and maid were not in residence and left, as was their custom, at seven. However, one of the papers, the *Ross Inquirer*, I believe, was more complete and noted the presence of a third occupant."

I registered amazement. "How could this fact go unrecorded elsewhere?"

"Ezariah Trelawney had a dog, Lama by name. The animal and the banker were inseparable. The old gentleman even took him to his bank office with him. Now I understand Constable Bennett's reference to the Silver Blaze affair."

"Of course," I said, with a flood of understanding. "The dog that didn't bark in the night."

"Dear me, Watson, that was but a trivial example of observation and inference. By the time you finished making our race horse adventure public, you had it sounding like a veritable triumph of deductive reasoning."

This mild chastisement bothered me not at all. Holmes consistently contended that I tended to overdramatize his superb reasoning powers. However, I knew that he secretly was delighted at having his *métier* appreciated and applauded.

"May I remind you, my dear Holmes, that no one else drew the inference that you did from the dog's behavior? Had you not, the great Silver Blaze might never have been found. But to return to the Trelawney affair, I see the similarity now. Since the dog, Lama, and his master were constantly together, no doubt the canine was in the murder room."

"He was. You will recall that the banker was seated and struck from behind. The outer doors to the house were not locked. Anyone might have entered, and the elderly gentleman could well have been dozing in his chair. But the prosecution will contend that had a stranger entered the house, the dog would have certainly alerted his master to the fact. However, Charles Trelawney was no stranger. Hence, it is the dog that may weave the rope that hangs him for murder."

This puzzled me. "My dear Holmes, instead of enjoying a quiet dinner we have two middle-aged men flying westward on what seems to be an open-and-shut case."

"Ah, but there is always a little more than meets the eye. I deduce this partially from items in the news accounts and also from the fact that Constable Bennett sent a plea for assistance. John Bennett, though buried in a backwater village, has carefully schooled himself in the latest methods of crime detection. I have carried on an intermittent correspondence with him for some time. He is alert and efficient. If he feels there are doubts and unresolved elements relative to this homicide, I am prepared to trust his instincts. Also, it would seem that the peaceful hamlet of Shaw was, in times gone by, the scene of deep-seated enmities and bloodshed. But these facets will be polished for us by the good constable upon our arrival."

When the train halted at the small station of Shaw, we were the only travelers to alight. A tall individual in a square-cut uniform coat with hat, who had been pacing the station platform, hurried to our side.

"Mr. Holmes," he said. "It is certainly a pleasure."

"It has been a while, Bennett," stated Holmes. "This is my associate, Dr. Watson."

Shaking hands with the constable, I wondered under what circumstances this country policeman and Holmes had met previously.

"I have rooms for you at the Queens Arms, which is our only inn hereabouts. It is but a short distance from here. The proprietor's wife is laying out a cold supper. Considering the time of your departure from London, I would imagine you could both do with a bite."

Bennett took the larger suitcase from me and led us down the street. In a short time we were in a pleasant room in the inn enjoying some excellent cold roast beef and a very tasty game pie.

Constable Bennett joined us in a yard of stout and lit up a cigar. As he ignited it and drew a first puff, he snatched the cigar from his mouth with an exclamation of surprise.

"How strange that I should decide to smoke this at such a time since it was a gift from the murdered man!"

"An Indian cigar," commented Holmes, "of the type rolled in Amsterdam."

"As to the murder, gentleman," said Bennett, "I trust the journals I sent provided some information."

"In outline form," was Holmes's response. "I was immediately intrigued by the fact that you were able to establish the time of death as between eight and ten on the fatal night."

"Fortunate happenstance," replied the constable. "At eleven, young Charles Trelawney came bolting out of his adopted father's house and almost ran into my arms. I was making a final round of the night just to make sure things were in order. I had just seen Dr. Devon Almont right here in the Queens Arms in the pub."

"Almont?" I asked with considerable surprise.

"He retired two years ago and came to live here," explained Bennett.

"I didn't know that. Naturally, I've read his articles in *Lancet* with great interest."

"You were fortunate, Bennett," stated Holmes, "to have one of the foremost pathologists in the world at your beck and call."

"I certainly beckoned," replied Bennett. "When young Charles told me that he had found Ezariah Trelawney with his skull crushed, I hightailed it over here and got Dr. Almont. Then the three of us returned to the Trelawney house. Doctor Almont checked the coagulation of blood on the back of the murdered man's head and tested the rigidity of the body and delivered the opinion that the murder had been committed between eight and ten."

"Almont's opinion would be accepted by any jury. In conjunction with Alexandre Lacassagne of France, he has made considerable contributions to the advancement of forensic medicine." Holmes thought for a moment. "If young Trelawney had just arrived from Hereford, he is in the clear, but I understand the stationmaster contested this."

Bennett nodded. "Pierce is a friend of young Charles, who is well liked by one and all. He saw the boy get off the last carriage of the six o'clock. A redheaded stranger and Charles were the only ones who got off the train. It meant nothing to him at the time, but at the inquest he had to tell what he had seen."

"Unwillingly," said Holmes. "That lends all the more credence to his words. Perhaps you had better relate what occurred, Bennett."

The constable's eyes narrowed, as though he did not wish to overlook a single fact.

"Charles was in a state of semi-shock, but after discovering the body, he had the presence of mind to close the door to the study before leaving the house. As I mentioned, the three of us returned there promptly. Upon opening the study door, we found everything as Charles had hastily related to me. Ezariah Trelawney was slumped in his chair in front of the fireplace. The right side of his skull was a sight indeed."

"The back of the skull, according to the newspapers," mentioned Holmes.

" 'Twas the back that got hit, but on the right side."

I shifted impatiently in my chair for it seemed they were splitting hairs.

"And the dog, Lama? He was still in the room?"

This point seemed of special interest to Holmes.

"Yes, sir," responded Bennett. "When Charles closed the door behind him, how could the little fellow get out?"

"That is my point, or at least a point of puzzlement." My friend chewed reflectively on a piece of beef. "Charles Trelawney testified that when he returned to his home, he found the door to the study closed. For his own sake, he might have said that the door was open. Had this been the case, the possibility could have existed that the dog was in some other part of the house when the fatal blow was struck."

"That bothered me also," replied the constable.

"Another thought," continued Holmes. "From your description and that in the papers, Trelawney's skull had been shattered from behind very severely. Would not a blow of such strength have driven the body from the chair?"

"Not necessarily," I stated automatically. "It was

mentioned that the corpse was well beyond the three score and ten. At that age, bones tend to become more fragile. The blow need not have been delivered with great strength."

"A good point, my dear Watson."

Bennett continued: "Whatever the weapon was, we did not find it. After inspecting the wound in greater detail, Dr. Almont delivered the opinion that it was caused by a club or stave perhaps, but definitely of wood. Lama was very nervous and whining, but Charles was able to quiet him. A book was on the floor, open, as though it had fallen from Ezariah's hands."

"Which it probably had," reflected Holmes.

"There was a half-consumed cigar in a tray by the chair. I believe that it was in the tray and lit when Ezariah was killed. It looked like it had gone out of its own volition."

"Now that is interesting," said Holmes. "I should have guessed the victim was a smoker since he made you a gift of a cigar."

" 'Twas the same type that I'm smoking right now," replied Bennett. "Ezariah had them sent to him from Amsterdam, as you divined, Mr. Holmes."

"What else can you tell us, Bennett?" asked Holmes.

"Well, sir, the maid and cook had left at seven, and a number of people saw them crossing the town square at that time. They both have families who testified that they returned home at their regular time and stayed there the entire night."

"So," said the great detective, "the murdered man was alone and someone, anyone, could have entered the house."

"For a fact," agreed Bennett. "We don't lock

doors in Shaw since crime, as such, really doesn't exist. Oh, occasionally a couple of sheep are missing but they always turn up. After payday, a few of our local cutups drain the bottle too deep and I have to make motions like a policeman, but that's about the whole of it. Until now," he added.

"But it was not always thus," prompted Holmes.

"Well, sir, now we go back a ways, long before my time. It was in the days of Monks Holes and the religious wars, and this was not the peaceful countryside it is now. Ezariah Trelawney was childless and adopted Charles, who was a foundling. There is another resident, Horace Ledbetter, who has a farm on the outskirts. He is the last of his family as well. He has a niece, Agnes Bisbee, who lives with him, but she is the daughter of his dead wife's sister and no blood kin. The local feed and grain store belongs to Vincent Staley, who never did marry. 'Tis said he has some relatives in Lancashire, but I don't know that for a fact. But it is a fact that at one time all three of the families were large ones and owned a lot of the land in these parts. It is hard to put a finger on what started it all. Some say that one of the Staleys was a wild lad with a taste for liquor and an eye for the lassies. He was supposed to have been riding through the countryside and come upon one of the Ledbetter girls and had his way with her. The next thing was the Staley estate was attacked in force by the Ledbetters and it was a pitching battle with a lot of bodies that never rose again. How the Trelawneys got into it is a mite vague. One story is that the oldest Trelawney tried to make peace between the two families and was cut down by mistake. Whatever the reasons, the three families went after each other with a vengeance. 'Twas like one of those

Scottish feuds one hears of that went on so long
that the original cause is unknown."

Holmes's lips were forming a comment when I
advanced an opinion.

"Possibly, you are referring to the Sutherland-
Mackaye feud, which continued for seven hundred
years. However, the cause is known. The two clans
went to war due to an argument as to which one
had been appointed by the king to defend the north
against the Dane. This local bloodletting sounds
more like the Hatfield-McCoy affair, which occurred in the southern United States. Or perhaps
the Lincoln County war, which was in the American West." I noted that both Bennett and Holmes
were staring at me in surprise as I amended my last
statement. "No, the Lincoln County cattle war was
of far shorter duration than the conflict you de-
scribe. However, it did produce William Bonney,
known as Billy the Kid."

Holmes's eyes seemed almost glazed. "Watson, I
never dreamed you were such a fount of wisdom
regarding feuds and family strife."

"Well . . . I . . . it just happened to be a subject that interested me at one time," I stammered,
somewhat embarrassed.

"Obviously," commented Constable Bennett. "In
any case, the Trelawneys and the Ledbetters and
the Staleys had a real go at it and the war
continued from father to son. When law finally
came, it was not a case of their drawing swords on
sight, but there were a lot of disappearances and
unusual deaths. Finally, they whittled each other
down so much there was not enough left to fight.
But it is a fact that Ezariah Trelawney, Horace
Ledbetter, and Vincent Staley hated each other
from childhood and their feeling did not mellow
with the coming of age."

"What a strange saga!" I said.

"But definitely connected with the death of Ezariah Trelawney. It gives us two potential suspects with more motive for murder than many assassins might have," was Holmes's comment.

Chapter 3

❧

The Blue-Eyed Dog

HOLMES SEEMED content with the preliminary review of facts. He rose, restlessly. Gone was the quiet thinker and logician of Baker Street, and instead there was the great detective intent on the chase. His eyes shone with a steely glitter and his whole body seemed to cry for action.

"The hour is late, but is it possible for us to examine the Trelawney house now?"

"I was hoping you would suggest it," answered Bennett. "I have been staying there to make sure that sensation-seekers don't disturb the premises."

Leaving the Queens Arms and crossing the town square, we found ourselves at the door of a stately mansion set well back from the tree-lined street. No lights were visible in the small village and the silence was broken only by the sound of night crickets and the infrequent hoot of a distant owl. As we approached the house, our arrival was acknowledged by excited barks.

"Lama," said Constable Bennett. "The maid will keep the place in trim until there is a disposition of the estate and together we try and take care of the little tyke."

As he unlocked and opened the outer portal, a small terrier with a long, heavy coat rushed out, continuing to bark. The little dog sniffed at Holmes's boots, and then mine, to learn what he could. Evidently, he detected nothing suspicious and preceded us into the house. As Bennett led me through the large hall toward a side door, Holmes paused to let the dog smell his hand and then took the liberty of stroking its long hair. Allowing Lama to show him the way, Holmes joined us in the room where Ezariah Trewlaney had breathed his last.

I admired the beautiful wood paneling on the walls of the study, which must have dated back to the time of Cromwell or before. Bennett carefully explained that nothing had been moved, though the maid had insisted on opening the windows and airing out the room. Nevertheless, I could still detect the acrid odor of the Indian cigars to which the deceased was evidently addicted. The study was a man's room with hunting trophies adorning the walls. An ancient suit of armor was standing in one corner.

Holmes inspected the chair in which Trelawney had been sitting, noted the attendant ashtray, and finally seated himself in the chair. An unusual affinity seemed to have sprung up between Lama and the great detective. After some urging and a couple of suggestive pats on his knee, Holmes was able to coax the creature onto his lap, where the little fellow made himself quite comfortable and appeared to sleep. Holmes remained immobile so as not to disturb the dog as he offered a suggestion.

"Let us recreate the crime casting you, Watson, in the sinister role of assailant unknown."

"As you wish, Holmes," I replied, knowing that

the little games that my friend chose to play frequently climaxed in amazing revelations. "What actions are called for in your manuscript?"

"You approach me from the door—stealthily, of course." I did so. "Now, I am sitting here, with a lighted cigar. I take a puff and place the cigar in the ashtray, with my right hand, as presumably, my left hand is holding a book."

"The fallen book was on the left side of the chair," interjected Bennett.

Holmes continued his fantasy. "Watson, you have a wooden weapon in your hand and you deliver a resounding whack to the back of my head." In dumb show, I followed directions. "Now," continued Holmes, "I presume that the path of the blow that you just delivered would bash me on the right side, since you happen to be right-handed."

"You are correct, Holmes," I agreed.

A keen glance from Holmes prompted Bennett to produce a pocket notebook, which he riffled quickly and then read from:

"The right occipital and parietal bones of the victim's skull were shattered by a blow from a heavy weapon." He flipped his notebook shut. "That was the statement of Dr. Devon Almont," he continued.

There was a sardonic smile on the detective's face.

"And, my dear Bennett, while you made reference to the Silver Blaze incident, I rather fancy that you considered another matter with which I was once occupied. May I hazard the guess that young Charles Trelawney is left-handed?"

The constable nodded, a gleam of admiration in his eyes. "I did not wish to muddle your thought processes with my own ideas, but you have arrived unerringly at the point that has bothered me."

"I'm delighted that you are both in agreement," I said, with a touch of asperity in my voice. "Would someone explain this to me?"

"'Black Jack of Ballarat,'" quoted Holmes. "Come now, Watson, if you were left-handed, would you have delivered the same blow that you just did in dumb show?"

"Of course not. How stupid of me." My mind flashed back to another time and a baffling mystery that had also taken place in rural surroundings. "But wait just a minute," I continued, prompted by another thought. "If Charles is ruled out as the murderer, we are left with Horace Ledbetter and Vincent Staley as suspects. Would the dog now dozing in your lap, Holmes, have allowed either of them to enter the house, much less this room, without raising a row?" I turned to Constable Bennett. "What breed of canine is Lama anyway? I don't recall ever seeing one like him before."

"Mostly terrier, I would imagine," was Bennett's answer. "A mixed breed."

"Let me disagree on that point," stated Holmes.

Suddenly, while gently stroking the subject under discussion, Holmes's lips pursed and he emitted a shrill whistle. The dog lay undisturbed on his lap.

"Good heavens, Holmes," I stammered. "What was that for?"

"Merely an experiment, old boy." Holmes's glance returned to Bennett. "As to Lama's ancestry, let me assure you that he is a pure-bred and blue-blood indeed. As Watson well knows, following the incident at Reichenback Falls, I placed myself in voluntary exile for several years, since two most vindictive enemies of mine, who were part of Professor Moriarty's gang, were still at liberty. During that period I traveled to Tibet and visited

Lhasa to confer with the head lama. Sitting in my lap, gentlemen, is a Lhasa Apso, also known as a Tibetan terrier. They are bred in that country as watchdogs. I suggested that the breed might be introduced to England, but others, more knowledgable on the subject, felt that our lowlands might not prove suitable to the strain. Anywhere in England is the lowlands to Lama here, since his native habitat is at sixteen thousand feet above sea level. However, our comparatively heavy atmosphere doesn't seem to have bothered this little chap, so perhaps my original thought was not without merit."

"This is all very interesting, Holmes," I persisted, "but you still haven't answered my question."

"The Lhasa Apso is peculiar in that it is the only dog, to my knowledge, that frequently has blue eyes. Oh, occasionally a Dalmatian may have one blue eye, but not two. Consider for a moment, both of you, how many blue-eyed dogs either of you has seen."

Bennett and I exchanged a glance and then a shrug. "I don't usually make note of the color of a dog's eyes," said the constable, "but I daresay you are right, Mr. Holmes."

"Both of Lama's eyes are blue," stated Holmes, as though this brought the matter to an end.

"For the life of me I fail to see what the little fellow's eye coloration has to do with this case." Possibly my tone was somewhat testy.

"Blue-eyed dogs are very subject to congenital defects, Watson. The most common one is deafness. Lama is as deaf as a post."

"But he barked his head off when we arrived."

"His sense of smell, dear boy, more acute in a canine than his sense of hearing. On the night of the murder, I picture Lama peacefully asleep at his master's feet in his soundless world. You noted, of course, that my shrill whistle of a moment ago did not even make him flinch. Trelawney was smoking one of his Indian cigars, the odor of which Lama has become unwillingly accustomed to through the passage of time. But the cigar smell effectively smothered the dog's ability to raise a scent. The acrid smoke anesthetized Lama's olfactory sense. Through no fault of his own, the poor dog was completely incapable of performing the task he was bred to do. Namely, to be a good watchdog."

"That does it," snapped Bennett. "I knew young Charles couldn't have been the culprit."

"Then we are back to Horace Ledbetter and Vincent Staley, both of whom suffer from congenital defects themselves. Namely, a blind hatred of each other and of Ezariah Trelawney."

"Very well put, Watson," said Holmes, with approval. "However, the hatred had existed for decades. What fanned the spark into flame at this particular time?"

"I can give you one theory, Mr. Holmes," said the constable. "In a village like Shaw, little happens that isn't public knowledge. Feed and grain is not the business it once was in these parts. Vincent Staley owed the bank a considerable amount. He had asked for an extension, which, due to Ezariah Trelawney, was denied. Staley is on the brink of ruin."

"Excellent, Bennett!" said the great detective. "Now you give us a motive." The sleuth of Baker Street was thoughtful for a time. "But we are still in the tender area of circumstantial evidence. How about Horace Ledbetter, the other prime suspect?"

"Just prior to the inquest, I rode out to his farm. His niece, Agnes Bisbee, said that the day of the murder she had had a conversation with Ledbetter which had thrown him into a rage and that he had ridden off to Marley. The Ledbetter property is midway between Shaw and Marley. I haven't had the chance to catch up with him since that time."

The constable concluded his statement with a hesitant air. Holmes regarded him searchingly, as though reaching within the recesses of his brain. "There is something else, obviously," commented the detective.

Bennett nodded. "It didn't come out at the inquest since it seemed to have no bearing at the time, but young Charles and Agnes Bisbee have been keeping company. They've had to be pretty sly about it too, considering the circumstances."

"Montague and Capulet." Holmes's eyes had a faraway look. "But, you see, it does explain a great deal. Charles Trelawney states that he returned to Shaw at ten forty-five and the stationmaster says he was on the six o'clock train. The young lover was silent because Romeo was with Juliet. Agnes Bisbee had a discussion with her uncle which threw him into a rage. About her intention to marry the stepson of his hereditary enemy, no doubt. The recent strain in the relations between Ezariah Trelawney and his stepson can also be laid at the doorstep of the star-crossed lovers."

Gently lifting the dog from his lap and placing him on the floor, Holmes rose to his feet.

"The hour is late, but the time spent has been profitable. I doubt if Charles Trelawney need appear before the magistrates or, indeed, the assizes."

"But there is a strong possibility that Vincent Staley might." Bennett's voice was grim. "Let me walk you back to the inn, gentlemen. You have indeed earned a mite of rest in what is left of the night."

While I had enjoyed a lengthy nap on the train

trip to Shaw, the country air acted like a soporific. It was late the following morning when I forced my eyes open to find Holmes, fully dressed, standing beside my bed, smiling. I grabbed at the watch, formerly the property of my departed brother of sad memory, which was on the bedstand. One look provoked a groan.

"Great Scott, Holmes, you have allowed me to sleep away the morning!"

"No matter, dear fellow. My expedition proved a simple one and required no assistance."

"Expedition, indeed," I said, climbing from the bed and dressing as rapidly as possible. "Where to, may I ask?"

"Marley, of course," replied Holmes. "You will recall that on the day of the murder, Agnes Bisbee said her uncle had ridden off to Marley in a rage. But Bennett stated that Ledbetter's farm was equidistant between Marley and Shaw. It occurred to me that Ledbetter might well have said he was riding to Marley but actually have directed his horse here."

"Placing him at the scene of the crime. And what, pray tell, did you learn in this adjacent hamlet?"

"Much more than I anticipated. Obviously, Agnes had informed her uncle of her love for Charles Trelawney. The news was such a shock to the old fellow that he rode into Marley like Rob Roy on the run. Leaving a foam-flecked horse, he promptly made for the only public house available and spent what was left of the early evening disposing of a complete bottle of very old Irish whiskey. This induced a certain truculence in his general attitude and the local constable was summoned. This protector of the peace, Farquhar by name, placed Horace Ledbetter with some difficulty in what our

American cousins call the local pokey. Ledbetter spent the entire night in a cell in the Marley jail."

"Good heavens!" I exclaimed, adjusting my waistcoat. "This gives Ledbetter an alibi."

"The very best I can think of, since it is supplied by the authorities themselves."

As Holmes helped me into my coat, there was a loud knocking on the door.

"Do come in," said Holmes, and the door opened revealing an agitated Constable Bennett.

"Forgive me, gentlemen," said Bennett, entering rapidly. "Things have taken a sudden turn."

"So Holmes has just told me."

The constable shot an inquisitive glance at my friend. "They said downstairs you had hired a four-wheeler early this morning. I was looking around town for you before coming here. Have you chanced upon something?"

" 'Twill wait," said Holmes with an airy gesture of one hand. "What have you learned, Bennett?"

"As you know, I have been staying at the Trelawney house to protect the evidence. This morning, I dropped by my digs and found an envelope under my door." Bennett extracted a piece of cheap paper from his pocket. "Let me read you the contents: 'Young Charles did not arrive at Trelawney's till just before eleven. Why don't you follow the finger of guilt, which points directly at Horace Ledbetter?'

"It's signed: 'One who knows,' " concluded Bennett.

"Your anonymous correspondent might just as well have affixed his name," said Holmes.

"My thought exactly, Mr. Holmes. Vincent Staley trying to implicate his enemy. I came here at once, but they said that you had already departed. Therefore, I went to Staley's home. There was no response to my knock, but I noticed the door ajar. Something prompted me to look inside and it's a good thing I did, gentlemen. I found Vincent Staley in his bedroom with his head bashed in."

"Good heavens!" This news set me back for fair.

"Hmmm!" added Holmes. "A turn of events I certainly did not foresee."

Bennett looked harassed. "I haven't made the fact known as yet."

"Just as well," was the detective's comment.

"I thought you gentlemen would accompany me to Ledbetter's farm. He is a tough old coot and I may need assistance in placing him under arrest."

I was dazed. "But he has an alibi."

Holmes explained the situation to Bennett. "Constable Farquhar of Marley assured me that Horace Ledbetter was under lock and key in the Marley jail the entire night of the murder of Trelawney."

Now it was the constable's turn to look dazed.

"Farquhar, eh? A good man. Bit of a local celebrity since he is our best dancer in these parts. Considered the master of the English Quick Step."

"Well, he has quick-stepped our only suspect right out of the picture."

"Not necessarily, my dear Watson."

"Half a moment, Holmes. Young Charles is innocent, being a left-handed man and incapable of delivering the death blow to his stepfather in the manner in which it was done. Staley has been murdered himself, and Horace Ledbetter has an ironclad alibi. Surely you cannot make anything sensible out of this hopeless tangle? Unless another suspect appears in a *deus ex machina* manner, we are at a hopeless dead end."

Holmes's eyes had narrowed thoughtfully. "The only way of arriving at what can be true is the careful elimination of what cannot be true. And there is a glimmer of light relative to this complex affair. Our solution lies in following your thought, Bennett, and departing immediately for the Ledbetter farm."

Using the four-wheeler that Holmes had secured for his trip to Marley, we were soon heading down a country road with Holmes at the reins. He set the horse at a good pace and it was not long before we pulled up in front of the substantial farmhouse that was our destination. We were met at the door by Agnes Bisbee, a comely girl with the creamlike complexion native to the locale. Her eyes were red from weeping.

"Agnes, we wish a word with your uncle," stated Bennett.

"He is in the barn," said the girl. "Though I don't know in what condition. The past few days have been a nightmare. He was gone all of one night and he's been drinking steadily and is up at all sorts of hours."

The recounting of recent events proved too much and she began to sob.

"Now, now," said Holmes with as close to a fatherly tone as he could come. "Things may not be quite as bad as they seem. Charles Trelawney will shortly be released from custody and his name cleared of any complicity in the heinous murder of his stepfather."

The girl's tears ceased at this news and Holmes indicated the barn.

"Now, if you will excuse us, I believe we can arrive at the end of this most regrettable chain of events," he said.

Holmes and I followed Bennett, who marched purposefully to the barn but found the door locked. He knocked authoritatively.

"Lea' me in peace," said a slurred voice from within.

"It is Bennett, Ledbetter. Open this door in the name of the law."

There was a silence for half a minute and then the sound of a bar being removed. Half of the large barn door slid open, revealing a gnarled man of six feet in height with a weatherbeaten face topped by a shock of white hair. He was dressed in work clothes. His callused hands and wide frame bespoke of strength and that durable power produced by hard manual labor.

I'm glad there are three of us, I thought. He looks as if he could be a bit of a handful.

The farmer indicated with a vague gesture for us to enter and turned inside and made his way to an anvil on which rested a depleted bottle and a tin tankard. He poured himself a considerable amount of whiskey and downed it in a gulp.

" 'Tis about Staley that I'm here," said Constable Bennett.

"Aye! I've been expectin' ya."

The farmer's eyes were bleary and his speech thick, but his brain appeared to be working. I surmised he had drunk himself sober, a physical peculiarity that has been known to happen.

"I'll no beat the bushes abaht it. 'Twas yesterday of an evening hour. I came out here in search of some bottles that I had hid away from Agnes's eyes. When I opened the door, there was Staley, curse his black heart! He was by the stalls with a club in his hand. I'd surprised him all right and he rushed at me. 'Twas all so fast. I grabbed this here fence rail what I had been workin' on." The farmer indicated a stoud piece of oak on the floor of the barn. "Wi' it, I blocked his first blow and swung. 'Twas a lucky hit or I would not be talkin' to ya now. Caught him full on the forehead, I did, and he was dead afore he hit the ground. What went through my poor addled pate then I canna tell ya. Somehow I were plagued with the idea of gettin' his carcass out of here, so I saddled my mare. She was skitterish, I tell ya, for she smelled Staley's blood, but I got him hoisted over her withers and into the saddle meself. Then I rode into Shaw and put the body in his house. I had the idea that if his corpse be found in Shaw, I would not be involved, but 'twon't work. I been livin' wi' the deed and that fierce moment for these hours past and it will nay do. I killed him."

With a groan, Ledbetter sank onto a bale of hay and buried his face in his hands.

"There seems to be ample grounds for a plea of self-defense," stated Holmes. "You said Staley had a club. Is it still here?"

Ledbetter just gestured toward a wall of the barn.

Holmes crossed to the indicated spot and secured a stave of seasoned wood, which he studied carefully.

"This, gentlemen," he continued, "will prove to be the murder weapon which did away with Ezariah Trelawney. The series of events seems clear. Impelled by blind rage, Vincent Staley stole into the Trelawney house and murdered his enemy. He felt that suspicion would fall on Ledbetter here, as well as himself, but when the authorities moved against young Charles, his plans went awry. Therefore, he left the anonymous messsage at your door, Bennett, where he knew you would find it, and then came out here with the murder weapon. He was in the process of concealing the weapon in Ledbetter's barn where it could be found without too much difficulty. However, being surprised in the act, he sprang upon Ledbetter with intent to kill."

Holmes turned his attention to the farmer.

"The fact that you have made a clean breast of the matter will carry considerable weight in court, my good man. While you do have the death of another human being to weigh on your conscience, the fact remains that Vincent Staley could have faced the same fate from the law, though by different means."

Chapter 4

❧

The Matter
of the Missing Gold

On our return trip from bucolic Shaw, Holmes was in excellent spirits, standard at the satisfactory conclusion of a minor case, and especially true if the solution was a rapid one. When a matter dragged on, my friend felt it a slur on his reputation and indulged in self-castigation for not having solved the puzzle sooner. As I have noted on more than one occasion, the life of a perfectionist is seldom tranquil. The matter of Ezariah Trelawney and the blood feud that had festered for so long in Herefordshire was patterned to his liking. A clear set of facts, an appearance on the scene followed by a rapid and satisfactory solution.

I was not prompted to share Holmes's carefree attitude, since the Trelawney affair ranked in my mind as the third in a row in which financial remuneration had not played a part. Not that our life or the machine that my friend had painstakingly constructed would be sore pressed. Holmes could secure an assignment—and at a dazzling fee—in a trice, but such was not his way. He relished the complete freedom to pick and choose among the problems that invariably beat a path to his door. Still, his expenses were enormous. In addition to our quarters, presided over by the ever patient Mrs. Hudson, there were at least four other domiciles he maintained around London, as a convenience in assuming various identities he had established. Five, if the house next door was included, since he owned it—and a most rewarding investment it had proven in one instance in particular. Then there was the staff at 221 B Baker Street as well as various specialists, mainly from the shadowland of the lawless, that he kept on retainers. If that were not enough, my intimate friend was known as an easy mark for some wayward soul attempting to rejoin the honest segment of society. Though his generosity in this respect was sharp-toothed. Woe be it to the former transgressor if he chose to revert to his previous way of life, for the specter of Holmes would be upon him like a mastiff on a hare.

It crossed my mind that I might curtail my wagers on equines that I fancied and make some moves toward reactivating my dwindling medical practice. The patients that still clung to me were a loyal group, but their ranks had been depleted. It occurred to me that I could well appeal to a more youthful group. Though my friend was most frequently pictured in the deerstalker and Inverness that he wore on our Shaw excursion, he was really a bit of a dandy. With his thin, whipcord frame enhanced by a tail coat and topper, we could have made something of a dashing pair had I possessed the strength of character to minimize my consumption of Mrs. Hudson's excellent fare or withstand the blandishments of the menus at Simpsons or the Cafe Royale. Along with thoughts of a stringent diet, I was entertaining the distasteful idea of abandoning my occasional billiard playing at

Thurston's when we arrived at our chambers and I learned that my thoughts regarding frugality were not necessary after all.

Holmes had dispatched a cable from Shaw alerting Mrs. Hudson to our time of arrival, as was his custom. This thoughtfulness proved of value. As we alighted from our hansom, Billy was, again, awaiting our arrival. Taking our valises, the page boy informed us that a visitor was, even now, in our chambers. Billy had developed an instinct for such things and brushed off our topcoats before we ascended the seventeen steps to our first-floor sitting room.

It was Claymore Frisbee who sat in the client's chair when Billy ushered us into our chambers. The president of Inter-Ocean Trust had had dealings with the great sleuth before and good reason to consult with him when troubled.

After cordial greetings and a minimum of small talk, Frisbee accepted my offer of liquid refreshment and got to the matter at hand.

"It is this gold bullion robbery, Holmes."

My friend's good-natured expression was promptly erased. Before he could comment, Frisbee beat him to the punch, no mean feat.

"I know of your meeting with Chasseur, but hear me out. You have to, you know," added the banker with a smile.

Curiosity struggled with the hauteur in Holmes's manner. "How so?"

"Have I not heard you say that to prejudge is the mark of a fool?"

Suddenly the sleuth chortled, something he did more often than people thought. "You have me there. Hoist on mine own petard. Let's hear your tale."

Holmes stirred up the fire in the grate with the

poker and then seated himself in the cane-backed chair, his long, sensitive fingers steepled together and his manner that of cordial attention.

"A special train of the Birmingham and Northern was routed to Great Yarmouth with a load of gold bullion to be shipped to France," stated the banker, accepting a glass from me. Knowing Holmes's habit of devouring the daily journals, he added, "I'm sure you're aware of the basic facts."

"Let us benefit by complete coverage," suggested Holmes, "including your involvement."

"I'll get to that," replied the banker. "There was half a million pounds on the B & N flyer and the line took elaborate precautions, but the robbery caught them by surprise."

Frisbee must have sensed a thought in Holmes's mind, for he paused in his narration and the sleuth did fill the void.

"I can't see why. Of all the articles of value used as a means of exchange, gold is the most anonymous. It lacks the serial numbers of currency and is devoid of geographical characteristics." My eyebrows must have elevated and the sleuth elaborated. "Gold mined in Australia or Russia is not a smidgen different from that found in Canada, the United States, or Africa. Nor does it matter how it is secured. Mined gold, panned gold, hydraulic gold, flotation gold; it is all the same. What surprises me is that more attempts are not made to steal it."

"Well, it is a mite heavy," said Frisbee, "and not available in large quantities outside of bank vaults."

"It was in this case," I said, taking my drink to the settee.

"An unusual situation," conceded the banker. "The precious metal was to be shipped to the Credit

Lyonnais in France. They have an issue of gold-bearing bonds coming due, and ever since their unfortunate investment in that Netherland-Sumatra swindle, there has been talk about their solidarity. The financial firm anticipated a considerable run on the bonds at due date with demands for payment in gold, so they strengthened their reserves by arranging a loan from a syndicate of our west coast banks that were well supplied. The metal was shipped to London from the banks involved and then placed upon the B & N special train. The B & N now employs one Richard Ledger for matters of this sort."

"I don't know his record," interjected Holmes.

"Former army. Service in India. He sold his commission and was taken on by the Kimberly interests as a security man. Comes well recommended. Ledger planned the shipment rather like a military campaign. He arranged for the flyer to make the run from London to Great Yarmouth non-stop. He had a solo locomotive out ahead of the train to prevent tampering with the tracks."

"With a means of communication should the advance engine come upon something, I assume," said Holmes, his attention definitely caught at this point in the story.

"A signal rocket," said Frisbee. "The treasure train consisted of an engine and two boxcars, with the gold in the second one, though that was a carefully guarded secret. On the roof of the first boxcar, Ledger had constructed a miniature block house with steel plating on the outside and slotted windows. Not a large affair, since he had to figure bridge clearances, but servicable. In it he had four marksmen whom he trained himself. Ledger has a considerable reputation as a dead shot."

"So we were told," I commented, and then wondered why I had spoken at all.

The banker continued: "The marksmen had an uninterrupted view of the sides and rear of the train, and Ledger stated that it was impossible for anyone to board the flyer once she was under way."

"A miscalculation, it would seem," said Holmes in a thoughtful manner. "These riflemen could not see the rear of the train from their fortified position, I would judge."

"No," replied Frisbee, "but the flyer never traveled at less than thirty miles per hour once clear of the B & N yards. To get to the rear of the second boxcar, hijackers would have had to approach from one side of the track or the other and been plainly visible."

"The entire trip being made during daylight?" I queried.

"It was planned that way."

Holmes rose suddenly and took a turn around the room, going over the matter with his quicksilver mind. Then he returned to the mantle and gazed moodily into the hearth fire.

"You might well take a shot at the newspaper game should banking ever bore you. You've described the matter far better than the journals."

"With more information," replied Frisbee modestly.

"What happened?" I asked, on tenterhooks.

"The bullion train was two hours outside of London and on an upgrade when suddenly smoke bombs were thrust through the slits in the riflemen's cubicle. They were blinded by the fumes and so choked that they could not even shout for help."

"And there being but one exit from their position, they were trapped within." The banker nodded in agreement with Holmes's remark, and the sleuth threw me a glance.

"Static warfare. Ineffective in modern times, Watson. The old feudal castles served their purpose but are antiquated now as is the entire enclave theory."

"But we're not discussing a military campaign," I remonstrated.

"The defense of the train was planned like one, and I would say the robbery had overtones of army tactics as well. In any case, we have the guard *hors de combat* momentarily . . ." Holmes turned suddenly toward Frisbee. "Was there any attempt to eliminate the riflemen?"

"None," replied the banker. "Whoever used the smoke bombs, and it had to be more than one person, effectively jammed the half-door leading into the armored cubicle and went about their business."

"Which was?" queried Holmes.

"They disengaged the rear boxcar from the train."

"You mentioned that this happened on an upgrade. The train continued up the slope and the boxcar rolled back down the track in the opposite direction."

"Fiendishly clever, wasn't it?" said Frisbee. "At the foot of the grade there was a stretch of level ground and an unused spur line. The boxcar rolled along until it came to the spur, which the thieves had switched. It then followed the feeder track until it came to a stop of its own volition some distance from the main line. There were marks of a wagon and horses there, and obviously they transferred the gold from the boxcar and made their escape."

"Aided, I judge," mused Holmes, "by the fact that

it took some time to discover how they made use of the abandoned spur line."

"That did slow up the pursuit," said Frisbee. "As soon as the robbery was made known to the engine driver and fireman, the locomotive went into reverse and there were signals all up and down the line. By the time they reached the station between the scene of the robbery and London, it was obvious that the missing boxcar had not come that way. Then someone recalled the old spur line, and the local constables, augmented by railway police, hurried back to it. By that time the wagon and the hijackers were long gone. Neighboring villages were alerted but nothing came of it."

Holmes had taken his cherrywood from the mantle and stuffed it with shag. Now he ignited it and puffed furiously. "Anyone," he said finally, "who could plan a theft so meticulously would not leave the disposition of the loot to chance."

He resumed his seat in the cane-back, gazing into the embers of the hearth fire. "See how they chose the place to strike. An upgrade, which would slow down the engine, but more important, bring the law of gravity into play. The rate of acceleration of the stolen boxcar had to be judged carefully. Too fast and it would derail itself. Too slow and it might not gain the momentum to carry it to the spur line and beyond. You did indicate that the railway car was found some distance from the main line, did you not?" he asked of Frisbee.

The banker nodded.

Holmes laid aside his pipe, and I sensed that he would embark on one of the recapitulations that he found so helpful. I was right.

"Two men at least reached the roof of the first boxcar. You mentioned smoke bombs, so I assume they were thrust through the rifle slots of the mobile blockhouse simultaneously and from both sides."

Again Frisbee agreed.

"With the riflemen temporarily out of action, they made their way to the rear of the boxcar and lowered themselves to disengage their prize from the rest of the train. Having uncoupled the connection, no difficult feat, they were now rolling downgrade with the freed bullion carrier. What would have been their next move?"

Frisbee had a ready answer.

"An iron ladder would allow them to gain the roof. It seems likely that they used it to arrive above the sliding door to the boxcar. One must have lowered the other down the side of the moving car to attack the door's fastening."

"By what means?" queried the sleuth.

"Cold chisel."

"Which requires a hammer. Which indicates two free hands, so the man was lowered by rope."

"I would think so," stated Frisbee. "By the time the boxcar had rolled off the main line, the job was probably complete and they were ready to unload."

"Aided by the third man," said Holmes.

"Where did he come from?" I asked.

Holmes patiently explained. "As soon as the treasure train passed the spur line, someone had to be there to activate the switch so the boxcar would leave the main line on its return trip. Then the third man closed the switch and took after the boxcar, on foot, I would imagine. By the time the boxcar came to a stop, the third man was available to aid in the unloading. One does not move a half million in gold in but a moment."

"Might there not have been more robbers involved?" I asked. It seemed a reasonable question.

"Not if I were planning it," said Holmes. "The more tongues, the more talk."

Again I blessed providence that my friend had not been born with a larcenous twist in his great brain. Had this been so, surely he would have made the infamous exploits of the late Professor Moriarty seem like something out of *Alice in Wonderland*.

Frisbee was eyeing my friend shrewdly.

"Inspector Stanley Hopkins was rushed to the scene from the Yard."

Holmes smiled. "Our friend Lestrade will be much put out I'm sure."

Frisbee continued: "Hopkins followed your line of thought regarding a member of the gang being positioned close to the spur line. He investigated that section closely but found no marks of a bicycle or horse."

"Then we can assume one of the thieves was fleet of foot." The detective's next question surprised me. "What was the original purpose of the spur line?"

"To service a tin mine that petered out a number of years ago."

"The boxcar came to a stop near the end of track?"

"Quite close to it." Frisbee let a silence grow, and then his eyes narrowed as he posed the key question. "What do you think?"

"I can give you a one-sentence summation," replied Holmes. "It is a pity that the security methods of the Birmingham and Northern were not planned as carefully as the robbery."

"Had they been, I would not be here," stated the banker laconically.

Holmes shook his head. "I fear your visit, as welcome as it is, has been for naught."

"We must talk of that."

"To no avail," said Holmes, and there was a note of finality in his voice. "You stated that you had heard of our encounter"—his eyes flashed to me for a brief moment—"with Alvidon Daniel Chasseur of the B & N. As a result of it, I vowed to have nothing to do with his stolen bullion."

"It's not really his problem," stated Frisbee. "Or his bullion either. Chasseur took on this gold transfer with an eye to future business. Shipments of special cargo. That's a nautical expression, but it has come to have meaning with land transportation as well. If the thing had worked smoothly, his armored-train idea might have caught on in other fields. However, that much gold in one place incurred a risk, so he took a policy on the shipment with our Inter-Ocean insurance division. If the gold isn't recovered, we stand to lose half a million pounds, the face value of our short-term coverage."

Holmes's manner had changed with Frisbee's words, but he stood by his guns, albeit in a less dogmatic manner.

"An investigation would involve my coming in contact with that man again . . ."

"Holmes, if we have to remit the insurance money, Chasseur's only problem is loss of face for having the bullion spirited out from under him. This matter has all the elements that I know you love so well. Take that Herefordshire banker Trelawney, for instance."

"Ezariah Trelawney?" exclaimed Holmes with a lightning glance in my direction. "What has he to do with it?"

"Trelawney arranged the consortium of west coast banks that provided the gold in the first place. Murdered, you know."

"We certainly do," I said forcefully.

Frisbee registered surprise at my vehemence but

shrewdly sensed that the wind had shifted and held his silence.

Holmes had risen again and unconsciously retrieved his cherrywood. Chewing on its stem, he stared into space for a moment before returning his intense gaze to Frisbee.

"Sometimes fate steps in," he stated. "All right, I'll take on the bullion case on behalf of Inter-Ocean Trust."

Chapter 5

∾

The Armored Train

ONCE MY FRIEND had committed himself, Claymore Frisbee hastened proceedings by the simple method of saying yes to everything. He seemed plagued by the fear that the great sleuth might change his mind. I could have reassured him on that point, for when Holmes decided on a course of action, he stuck to it with the tenacity of the English bulldog. The banker agreed to arrange an appointment with Richard Ledger, the B & N head of security, and while Holmes was gazing out the bow window considering other necessary lines of investigation, Frisbee handed me an unmarked envelope that had to be a pre-prepared persuasion ploy.

I could guess what it contained. Holmes's habitual reserve was most apparent in his reluctance to consider or discuss money, an enduring neurosis of the English upper middle class. Frisbee, who knew his man, had written a generous check for expenses to nail down the detective's involvement in the bullion problem. Regardless of his motive, I mentally thanked the banker, for this case gave indications of a widespread search and Holmes was sure to involve what his brother, Mycroft, referred to as the "rag tag army" at his command. When deputizing the shadowland group he used, Holmes seemingly gave no thought to expenditures. However, his methods were not as Croesus-like as might seem at first sight. The most precious commodity in the sleuth's opinion was time. "Who can place a price, Watson, on an hour?" he was wont to ask on occasion, and I must admit that my native frugality could find no response to this.

After the departure of Claymore Frisbee, Holmes was at the desk, a sheaf of foolscap at his elbow and a quill pen in his hand. I knew that Billy would be summoned shortly and dispatched to the cable office with communiqués, and throughout London, and in other places as well, the machinery of the great sleuth would grind into action.

Prior to dinner, he revealed some of the thoughts coursing through his superb mind. This delighted me, since it was not a customary procedure so early in the game. It crossed my mind that the bullion robbery being a major coup of the lawless, Holmes must have anticipated being drawn into it. Perhaps he was already more *au courant* with the matter than I had thought, and indeed, he might have made some plans as to his initial moves before the summons from the B & N Railroad or the entrance of the Inter-Ocean Trust upon the scene.

"Our first step, I fear, will be in a fruitless direction," he stated with a wry smile. "No matter, we must make it."

"Where is the gold?"

He threw me a surprised glance. "Quite right. The *raison d'être* of the robbery is no small matter, and one does not just toddle around town with that much precious metal in one's pocket. It has to be stored somewhere."

"Your thoughts being that the gold might guild the path to the culprits."

Again he registered faint surprise. "Right on, old chap. What other thoughts do you have in mind?"

It was my turn to be surprised. Usually Holmes revealed his ideas almost as though speaking to himself. My questions and comments were the rhythm background to his analytic violins, a *lietmotif* of the Holmes symphony. Now, with the baton thrust into my hand, I was at a momentary loss but determined to wave it in some direction if only to make my presence known.

"We are not wanting for a motive," I said. "Greed inspired by the rare substance that has driven men to desperate deeds throughout history."

"Or need," responded Holmes dreamily. "A beggar might purloin a shilling for fish and chips and a night's lodging, whereas one higher on the social ladder, beset by obligations he cannot meet, risks disgrace for a greater sum."

"The motive being the same despite the difference in the value of the stolen object," I echoed.

"Exactly. Please continue, Watson."

Drat it, I thought. The ball is back in my court.

"You mentioned, Holmes, how well the robbery had been planned. Does that not indicate a knowledge of the terrain and of railway procedure?"

"A shrewd thrust, that last part."

"Not too revealing, however. Any number of people could have a working knowledge of the B & N."

" 'Twould not suffice. It was a special train that was attacked and it ran on a schedule created for it. Normal procedure had little to do with the bullion carrier."

He had me there and I thought furiously. "Isn't a key problem the means by which the thieves got on the train? A lot of thought had gone into preventing just that from happening."

"Considering that our problem involves a train, I will resist the impulse to say that you are on the right track, old fellow."

Encouraged, a thought came to me. "Let us assume that the riflemen guards were not part and parcel of the plot."

"I'll accept that."

"Then once the freight achieved running speed, it would seem more than difficult to get aboard."

"Agreed."

"Then the thieves rode with it from the start."

"Not an unwieldy theory at all. Really, Watson, you have developed the ratiocinating mind through our long association."

This being rare praise indeed from Holmes, I plunged ahead. "Is there not an expression common in America, 'riding the rods'?"

"Relates to traveling hobos."

"Quite. Could not the two men you picture have been hidden under the boxcar before the engine assumed motion?"

"A possibility. How they would manage to crawl from their place of concealment and gain the roof eludes me, but the inventiveness of the homo sapiens is limitless."

"The only other thought that comes to mind is that the thieves hid themselves within the boxcar, but that idea is self-defeating as they would have been unable to get out of the securely locked carrier."

"Your first thought is the one that will bear investigation, good fellow."

At this point Mrs. Hudson made her presence known. It was time for dinner. This was the day of a most important social gathering, the meeting of the

Marylebone Sewing Circle. While the event did not
warrant a squib in the *Evening Chronicle*, it was
dear to our landlady's heart. To make amends for
her absence from the premises, Mrs. Hudson fairly
outdid herself. We were served consommé Marie
Stuart and filets de sole Carlton. Then we had thick
mutton chops, their ends curled around a broiled
kidney and affixed with a toothpick. This led my
mind to the subject of claret and I brought forth a
bottle of Château Lafitte '68, which I had been
saving. By the time we dealt with a toothsome
soufflé auz pêches à l'Orientale, the evening, in my
mind, was a merry occasion indeed.

Following our repast, it was my thought to
peruse an article in the latest *Lancet*, but I soon
found myself nodding over the medical journal.
With apologies to Holmes, I soon made my way to
bed and promptly fell into a deep sleep. On this
night, with a nod no doubt to the Château Lafitte,
bottled on the estate, I had no dreams of great
trains hurtling through the night to their doom.
The next thing I knew there was a shaking of my
shoulder. As my eyes reluctantly blinked open, I
beheld Sherlock Holmes leaning over my bed with
a half smile on his lips. It was a new day.

"Come, old chap, if you would be part of the
opening act of this drama we have become entan-
gled in."

Despite a delightful lassitude, the coldness of the
room and the floorboards, and the reticence of
protesting bones to assume motion, I mumbled
something to my intimate friend and made haste to
perform my morning ablutions and struggle into
clothes. In our sitting room, the smell of Holmes's
pipe was everywhere. I gave it scant heed as I
eagerly siezed the cup of coffee he poured from the
great silver urn and then applied myself to that

mainstay of the empire, a stout English breakfast. The sleuth might have been up all night for all I knew, though I noted no clues as to the presence of others. As I wolfed kippers and eggs, he was going over a sheaf of papers that had the appearance of a business report.

When I poured myself a second cup of coffee and ignited a morning cigarette, Holmes tossed the document on the desk surface and joined me.

"My brother is a most meticulous man," he commented, "and despite his bulk, fast-moving. I cabled him last night for a report on recent transactions on the gold market, and early this morning a complete dossier came to our doorstep. I sometimes wonder when he sleeps."

"A thought that has bothered me at times relative to you," I replied, downing the last of my repast.

"The normal human requires sleep to oil the mechanism and food to fuel it, old friend," stated Holmes. "A thinking machine does not operate in that fashion."

Holmes often declared that he was a walking brain, since thinking was his sole reason for being, and I humored him by pretending acceptance. The fact that he was a superb fencer and the finest amateur boxer I had ever seen prompted me to adopt a different view, though I was the first to agree that he wasn't normal.

He did not seem disposed to divulge any results of the past evening, so I posed an obvious question. "What move do you plan now?"

"We meet with that Ledger chap at the B & N freight yard in half an hour, Watson. The gold train is there, and possibly we will find clues to buttress your theory of robbers 'riding the rods'."

It was an overcast day and a chill wind faced us

as we hailed a hansom and made for the freight yards. The vicinity we sought had the bleak, forlorn look exhibited by portions of London in the early morn. Holmes seemed to know exactly where we were to go. When we alighted from our conveyance, he set off at a brisk pace that I struggled to match. Richard Ledger was awaiting our arrival beside the office of the freight dispatcher. His thin face had the bronze cast of one oft exposed to the sun and there were deep circles under his bright eyes, which were a peculiar shade of light blue. His manner toward Holmes was most deferential, but then he had worked for the Kimberly people and the diamond syndicate was not known to hire dullards.

"The train is over here, Mr. Holmes," he said after suitable greetings. Assuming that Holmes's prime interest was in the carrier, he turned and walked through the maze of intersecting roadbeds, and we found ourselves beside an engine and two boxcars on a short section of rail that Ledger referred to as a hold track.

Claymore Frisbee's description of the bullion carrier had been accurate, and I noted nothing that I had not expected to see. While Holmes and Ledger conversed beside one boxcar, I walked around the train, intent on an investigation of my own. Atop the boxcar nearest the engine was the specially constructed fortified position looking rather like a pillbox. It seemed small for four riflemen, but I was interested in the line of sight afforded by the slots in the armor plating of its sides. It did not take long to establish that the marksmen could cover everything save for a thirty-five-degree arc centered at the rear of the second boxcar. The rifle roost, for want of a better term, would have suggested the turret of the U.S. Navy's monitor-type vessel had it been round rather than square. I bent down to survey the undercarriage of the boxcars and found myself regarding Ledger and Holmes on the other side of the track.

"It could have been done, Watson," said Holmes. Then he threw a quick remark at Ledger. "A theory of my associate." The sleuth's intense eyes returned to me. "They might have secured themselves by the rear wheels, though it would have been a perilous and most uncomfortable journey. But what about their equipment? The smoke bombs, hammer and cold chisel and small arms as well, in case the plan went awry?"

I nodded in agreement with his words and hastened around the rear of the train to rejoin the sleuth and the security man. When I arrived on their side, Holmes had evidently explained my thought to Ledger.

"Impossible, Mr. Holmes," Ledger was saying. "Before the gold shipment took off, I went over the undercarriages and the boxcar interiors myself. The train left here with no one aboard save the engineer and firemen and my guards." As Holmes nodded and I drew up by the two, Ledger continued: "The riflemen were all bonded and of good reputation. Two are formerly of the Lincolnshire Regiment."

"I know," said Holmes, and I later wondered at this remark. "We'd best have a look at the roofs, for that's where the mischief started."

Ledger led us to the rear coupling between the two boxcars and we carefully mounted an iron ladder. On the top of the second boxcar, which had held the gold, Holmes went to his knees to survey the roof with his ever-present pocket glass. I noted that he paid special attention to the right aft section above the sliding door in the car's side. I began to pose a question, but he shrugged and then his long legs took him forward on the roof to the edge and he leaped from there to the first boxcar with Ledger agilely following. I contented myself with climbing down the ladder we had mounted and up the matching one to the top of the adjacent car. A more dignified approach and more fitting for an overweight middle-aged general practitioner. I had no desire to secure the services of a fellow physician for treatment of a break or contusions.

Close to, the gun emplacement revealed nothing that I had not noted from a distance and Holmes seemed to be paying it scant attention. He was inspecting the top of the boxcar and gestured for Ledger to join him on the forward end nearest the engine.

He had risen and was pointing toward a streak of white paint running across the boxcar roof.

"Was this marking in some way connected with your security measures?" he asked.

The youngish man shook his head. "Mr. Chasseur originally had a rectangular area marked in paint as the position of the guard house. I indicated to him that the line of fire would be improved if it was built farther back, to which he agreed. Evidently, the man who was to paint out the line only completed a part of his job. We were in a bit of a rush to get the train ready, you know."

Holmes accepted this without question, but I noted that he positioned one heel on the mark and strode back past the armor-plated cubicle to the end of the boxcar. Holmes could suit his stride to an exact three feet and I knew he was measuring a distance, though for what reason I could not fathom. Nothing else about the train claimed his attention, so we descended to the ground, where Holmes evidenced a considerable interest in our guide.

"How long were you with the diamond people?" he asked.

"Three years. The mines are not as they once were, which made my duties easier. They are now walled compounds with more guards per acre than a military base. Getting in and out is about as easy as getting close to the Crown jewels. To mount a raid would take a trained military unit and a sizeable one at that. Therefore the main duty, in addition to maintaining an alert guard force, was inspection of the native diggers when they period- ically left the compound to rejoin their tribes in the interior. It's all been rather worked out by formula. Prior to departure, an enema is used to make sure a diamond doesn't go out in someone's intestines. Anyone leaving is stripped to the buff and doctor- inspected, the interior of his mouth as well."

"Necessary, I suppose," commented Holmes. "What brought you back to England?"

"A friend of Mr. Chasseur is a major shareholder in Kimberly and must have given me a spanking recommendation. The B & N had some problem with warehouse thefts and I was offered my present position. Jumped at it, I might add. Africa is all very well, but the boredom of the job was getting to me."

"I can imagine. Where did the robbery take place?" asked Holmes, suddenly shifting subjects.

"Outside of Brent. A small village almost due north of Colchester."

We were back by the dispatcher's now, and as Holmes thanked Ledger for his trouble, a thought burst upon me.

"I say, we've rather dismissed the idea of the thieves being aboard the special when it pulled out. But I noted a blind spot at the rear of the train. Might they not have somehow overhauled the train as it was leaving the yards?"

Again it was Ledger who supplied the cold water.

"The special was routed on the main line," said the security man.

"To be red-balled through," added Holmes.

"Exactly." There was a small smile on Ledger's tight mouth, as though in recognition of Holmes's familiarity with railroad jargon. "Along with a group of trusted employees, I was right here to watch her off, and she'd gained considerable speed by the time she was out of our sight. They got to her beyond the yards, Dr. Watson, or a whole group of us had better have our eyes checked."

"Certainly not necessary in your case," said Holmes, and I noted that Ledger shot him a quick glance. The comment did seem cryptic at first, but then Ledger was relatively young and one could assume that his eyes were keen.

"You did not decide to go with the bullion, and I have wondered why." Holmes's voice had hardened slightly.

"Mr. Chasseur had an appointment with the people at the London, Tilbury and Southend Railroad. After that, we were to go together by express to Yarmouth to be present when the gold was loaded aboard a channel boat."

He paused for a moment with a wry expression. "The news of the robbery reached us before we left, so the trip to Yarmouth had no meaning. My employer rather left this matter in my hands and I've let him down for fair. If there's anything I can do to help in your insurance investigation, please call on me."

Noting Holmes's sudden and sharp glance, he elaborated quickly. "I know where the request for me to meet you here came from, sir. It's not hard to judge what rekindled your interest in this matter."

Holmes seemed kindly disposed toward Ledger's frankness. At least he did until we had regained a hansom and were clattered back toward Baker Street.

"What did you think of him?" he queried.

"Seemed forthright enough. After seeing the special freight, can't say I'd fault his plan for guarding it either."

There was a twinkle in Holmes's eyes. "The former lieutenant in the Grenadiers was not guilty of falsehood," he said.

"What then? Something is amiss or you would not be discussing him."

"You know me too well, old friend. We had visitors after you were abed last night. I learned that there is another facet to Ledger's career that he did not choose to mention—his feats of marksmanship."

"We'd already heard of that from two sources."

"But not of Alvidon Chasseur's involvement with the Wellington Gun Club."

I was regarding Holmes blankly, and bless him for not letting the matter drop, an annoying habit he had on occasion.

"Industrial tycoons are not rushing down to Sussex or similar country areas for long weekends as in times gone by. Pressure of business, you know. With fox hunting and grouse shooting on the wane, they have found release for competitive spirits and an interest in ordinance by forming gun clubs, where target shooting occupies the members. The clubs all have rifle teams and they compete in a league, which may explain the number of former members of Her Majesty's forces being employed by big business."

"Ahhh," I said. "Now I understand your remark about the man's vision."

"Ledger's reputation assures us that he has the eyes of an eagle."

"And a position was created for the shootist so that he could represent the Wellington Gun Club," I continued, feeling on firm ground.

"He's qualified in his job, I'm sure," replied Holmes, "but his offer of employment was certainly based in part on his marksman abilities. The Wellington Club has the champion rifle team of greater London and will defend their title in the near future against the Bagatelle Club, sponsored by Lord Balmoral. It might be fitting if we attended that match, Watson."

I did not have much time to consider this matter since we had returned to our chambers and Holmes was occupied reading cablegrams and several letters delivered to our door. He then wrote out answers and casually informed me that he would be off to Essex by the afternoon train and would appreciate my company if I felt so disposed. As he summoned Billy to deliver his queries and instructions to the cable office, I thought again how the sleuth had shunned the installation of a telephone in our quarters. In matters of criminal investigation, Holmes was ultramodern and I'm sure his many innovations must have influenced Sir Bernard Spilsbury, the forensic medicine genius, in later years. Why Holmes did not choose to use Mr. Bell's greatest invention I could not guess, though its absence never seemed to hamper one of his investigations.

The village of Brent being in Essex, the sleuth was going to visit the scene of the crime, and nothing would keep me away from that. It was apparent that whilst I had been the slug-a-bed the previous night, my friend had used the time to good advantage. From long experience, I knew I would just have to wait to find out what else he had learned.

Chapter 6

❧

End of Track
with Dandy Jack

WE REACHED Brent on a local and, to my surprise, found a four-wheeler plus driver awaiting our arrival. Holmes approached the conveyance with confidence.

"You would be Dandy Jack," he said to the driver.

"Not by that name in these parts, sir," responded the man, saluting briefly with his whip. His broad face was creased by a toothy grin.

"And my name is not Sherlock Holmes," responded the sleuth, "nor is this gentleman with me Dr. Watson."

"What goes in one ear comes out t'other, sir. That way it don't come out the mouth."

During this singular conversation, Holmes and I entered the carriage, which swayed back slightly as our posteriors found the straw-stuffed cushions. The driver's whip flicked lightly on the rump of a sturdy bay and we were off. Holmes offered no directions nor did the driver seem to require any.

In contrast to the city, a limpid sun tried to brighten the rural scene and succeeded in part, though the air was crisp and cold. In London, with the moisture of the Thames close-by, I would have thought it raw, but not so in the dry and clear air of the countryside. Leaving the buildings of the village of Brent was a matter of a moment, and as we were setting a brisk pace, it was not long before I spied a ribbon of rails in the distance.

"Now if you was that amacheur peeler wot you mentioned," said the driver, "you might be interested in the spur line where they hit the bullion train. People hereabout are talking 'bout nothin' else, the robbery bein' the biggest thing wot's happened in Brent, you see."

"It does seem the place to be for a casual visitor," said Holmes. "I take it the rails ahead are on a straightaway and the roadbed follows an upgrade in that direction." Holmes was indicating to our right, where the rails curved around the base of a small hill.

Dandy Jack turned to view us and his face again was transformed by a grin. It changed a weathered and potentially grim visage dramatically.

"Right, sir."

"How far up the grade is the bridge?"

Since no such feat of engineering was visible as yet, I well understood the expression of surprise on Jack's face.

"You've been here before," he said with sudden understanding.

"Never to my knowledge," replied Holmes.

"Then 'owd' you know . . ." Our driver's voice dwindled out and he shot another glance over his shoulder. There was a shrewd look in his eye.

"Guess you're as good as they say, all right. There is a bridge, sir, as you shall shortly see. I take it that's what you're interested in."

"For the moment." The matter dropped there. I felt prompted to inquire of Holmes but chose to follow the driver's example. My friend would have probably responded with one of his pet phrases like, "It had to be, old fellow," which seemed to explain everything to him but was of scant use to me.

Dandy Jack guided his four-wheeler in a zig-zag course through country lanes and soon we were riding adjacent to the rails and around the curve. Ahead loomed a vehicular bridge necessitated by a main road stretching south to Colchester, I assumed.

When we reached that point in the lane closest to the bridge, our driver reined in the bay and helped us down from our seats. Holmes requested Dandy Jack to accompany us, and he secured the horse's reins to a tree and caught up quick enough as we made our way across pastureland to the bridge. Holmes followed the roadbed under the overpass, his eyes surveying the span above us, and then we were on the other side. My friend seemed to be measuring the distance from the tracks to the top of the overpass and then he cast his eye around the open ground surrounding us on both sides. In the season this portion was tilled and for this reason Holmes spied what he was looking for. It was a straight length of wood that was quite dead and tapered at one end. Formerly a bean pole, no doubt, that had been thrown aside because of the brittleness of the old wood. Evidently it would serve Holmes's purpose, for he secured it and brought it to the point of the roadbed directly under the edge of the overpass. Measuring with his eyes, he whipped a handkerchief from the pocket of his traveling ulster and tied it to the pole. Needless to say, Dandy Jack and I were regarding him with some mystification.

As he righted the pole under the bridge, he did

offer an explanation. "From here to the handkerchief represents the height of the boxcar from the ground."

"What about the armored cubicle?" I exclaimed, with a sudden idea as to what he was about.

"That does not figure in my calculations." Holmes indicated for Dandy Jack to hold the pole in the position he had placed it and stepped back, his eye swiveling from the handkerchief to the top of the bridge. "Hmmmm, about seven feet to the under portion of the span and another five feet to the parapet of the bridge. A bit more distance than I had figured, but it could be done."

Positioning himself directly underneath the edge of the bridge, he marched down the track with his measured stride for a short distance. He then stopped, turned, and gazed at the top of the bridge, nodding in seeming satisfaction. Returning, Holmes gestured for Dandy Jack to lower the pole, and he retrieved his handkerchief from it.

"Is that the shortest way to the bridge?" he asked, indicating a sharp slope to the south of the tracks.

Open-mouthed, our driver nodded.

"But a moment, gentlemen, and I will rejoin you," said the sleuth, making for the hillside. As he swarmed up the incline with no apparent difficulty, Dandy Jack sidled over toward me, all the while watching Holmes's figure with a somewhat alarmed expression.

" 'E don't say much, does 'e?"

"On the contrary, he can be quite loquacious," I replied with, I fear, the smugness of one dealing with a familiar subject. "It's just that he's a bit hard to understand," I added.

"That I can believe," the man growled.

"It is all very plain to him," I exclaimed somewhat defensively.

Dandy Jack's grin came to the rescue of his bafflement.

" 'Tis glad I am, sir, that it's plain to someone."

This seemed to cover the subject and we remained silent until Holmes returned shortly thereafter. I noted, with envy, that he was not even breathing deeply.

"Back to the carriage, lads," he ordered, and there was a pleased expression on his usually inscrutable features. Dandy Jack and I followed the sleuth's long strides. When we reached the four-wheeler, Holmes had a question.

"How close can you get us to the spur line?"

"Iffen I goes 'round by the old mine, I can drive right to the end of it," was Dandy Jack's reply.

"Capital. The junction of the feeder line with the main track has little to tell us," said Holmes.

"First time I knew rail track could tell me anythin'," said Jack, and promptly lapsed into silence. I sensed there was something about Holmes that made him nervous.

Our route involved a number of turns and the gentle curves that country roads are prone to have, and I completely lost any sense of direction. When we arrived at a cleared area with several boarded up and dilapidated wooden buildings, a rail bed that ended at a sizeable pile of boulders relocated my directional bug. The spur line went in a straight northeast direction, placing the main line in my mind. The clearing had been hewn from a heavily timbered area, and already, second growth was making a considerable showing. A small hill close to the end of tracks was studded with rocky outcroppings and there was a sizeable opening in its side, now shielded by loose rock. This had to be the abandoned tin mine.

While Holmes was busy scrutinizing the ground around the termination point of the spur line, I walked closer to the mine entrance. It seemed that wooden supports within had finally given up the ghost. Action of rain and weather had resulted in a cave-in at the mouth of the digging. A small boy might have worked his way within, but I certainly could not, nor did I wish to, for another shifting of the hillside might have entombed me. I was glad to rejoin Holmes, who had straightened from the semi-crouch in which he had been inspecting the area. Words were unnecessary. His manner told me that any clue that might have been seduced by his uncanny powers of observation into a thin thread of revelation and thence into fabric for a garment of truth had been taken or trampled by the heavy-footed minions of the law who preceeded us to this spot.

Never at a loss in finding other avenues of investigation, Holmes brought his attention to bear on Dandy Jack, he being the expert on the locale.

"The boxcar was found right at the end of track?" he asked that worthy.

An affirmative nod was the reply.

"An uncanny bit of figuring," said the sleuth, and then chose to confide in our driver.

"The boxcar with the gold was separated from the rest of the train on the upgrade. Gravity caused it to roll backward, picking up enough speed to carry it to the spur line and then right here. How far would you say?" he asked, regarding Dandy Jack intently.

"Good half mile." Drawn into the recreation, the man contributed another thought after a moment.

"If the freight carrier was goin' a mite fast, those

rocks would have stopped it." He indicated the boulders I had noted earlier. "Though I don't recall a mention of one end bein' bunged in. There's a slight downgrade in the spur line, which you've noticed."

Holmes indicated that he had.

"They could ha' levered her here had they wished. A coupla stout timbers would ha' done it."

"And stout backs." My friend seem dissatisfied. "But why when they could just as well have driven the wagon to wherever it stopped? It was a wagon, wasn't it?"

His keen eyes had never left Dandy Jack.

"Aye. Iron-tired wheels. The tracks was plain when the railroad police and Constable Sindelar got here from Brent."

"You heard about it." Holmes's statement had the overtones of a question.

"I come later to 'ave a peek. 'Twas but one wagon, two horses."

"It was a heavy load. All right, Jack, what would you have done with half a million in gold ingots?"

"Different from them, it would have been. A wagonload of hay outward bound in one direction. Some feed bags in another. The safest of the lot, a load of manure, taking a third route."

"With gold ingots riding under the loads," said the sleuth, nodding as if in agreement with this idea.

"Might they not have done that? Divided the booty further along the line?" Holmes then suggested.

Dandy Jack's denial was firm. "There was not that much traffic at the time. I know pretty much everybody hereabout. Iffen it was outsiders, somebody would have noticed them."

"There were no locals involved. You're sure of that?"

"Very sure, Mr. Holmes." This was the only time Dandy Jack used my friend's name and a flicker in his guarded eyes showed that he regretted it. There was no reaction from my friend at this breech of etiquette. Rather, he seemed prepared to accept Dandy Jack's statement.

"Then how did they do it with but one wagon?"

Our driver shrugged. " 'Tis a point that's puzzled me."

"From a professional standpoint," said Holmes dryly.

Suddenly the sleuth whirled and set out toward the main line, his long strides eating up distance. Dandy Jack and I looked at each other for a moment questioningly, and then I shrugged and followed in Holmes's footsteps with our driver by my side. My judgment of distance is faulty, but it seemed like less than a quarter of a mile hike to the main line, where we found Holmes inspecting the junction point with his magnifying glass. Arising, he brushed off his knees. A look at Dandy Jack evidently carried a message and the man secured a metal bar from a wooden box beside the track. Using it, he activated the switching mechanism and I noted the iron tracks shift. Holmes reached down with a finger and straightened to rub it against his thumb.

"Well oiled, but they would do that."

"The man positioned here, you mean, after the gold train went by," I exclaimed.

"Or before, for that matter." The sleuth's attitude was casual and he seemed to have lost interest in the matter.

Our walk back to the four-wheeler was made in silence. I had nothing to say nor had Dandy Jack, who had recovered his grin. Holmes was deep in thought, his hands clasped behind his back and his aquiline face chin down on his chest. In the conveyance, Dandy Jack headed back to Brent since there were no orders to do otherwise.

As we approached the small village and its station, Holmes summoned himself from his reverie.

"I would appreciate your thinking more on how that wagonload of gold was removed with no one the wiser. In daylight too, for the authorities found the boxcar before night fell."

Dandy Jack indicated that he would give the matter due consideration, but there was little enthusiasm in his manner. Why our driver should be expected to come up with an answer eluded me. At the station, Holmes passed some bills to Dandy Jack, who did not bother to count them before shoving them into a pocket with a gesture of acknowledgment that could have doubled for thanks.

As he stood on the platform and waved us goodbye, did I detect an expression of relief on his weathered face?

On the train, I viewed Holmes with purpose. I had allowed him a lengthy period for meditation, and enough was enough. Questions were bubbling on my lips. I never had the chance to ask them; Holmes divined my thoughts.

"Dandy Jack has led a not uneventful life, and it was fortunate for our purposes that he was on the scene." Holmes removed his ostrich-skin pouch and fueled his short-stemmed briar. "For that matter, the sleepy village of Brent has seen more exciting times. It was once the halfway house for a thriving business." My mouth opened with the obvious question, but Holmes continued: "A ring of brandy smugglers got their contraband cargo this far and then sent it in various directions, much in the manner that Dandy Jack mentioned."

"He was, then, a part of the ring?"

"Very good at his job, too."

"How do you know of this, Holmes?"

"I broke the ring."

"Ah, then you knew Jack."

"Only by reputation. There was a falling out among the thieves. The matter of greed you mentioned previously. There were two casualties, which did not sit well with one member of the gang. I was able to contact him, by post actually, using a code name. We transacted some business, always by the mails. The entire gang was captured, including a customs official in Yarmouth."

"But they didn't all go to jail," I said with a wise smile, which his answer erased.

"Actually, they did. However, one of the gang escaped after a brief period in a certain penal institution. He's never been found."

Holmes puffed on his pipe for a considerable moment, his eyes harkening back to times gone by. Then he continued in a low tone of voice which, on occasion, served as a tocsin for a confidential matter of importance.

"Dandy Jack is a singular name and rather hard to forget. Old friend, we'd best forget it just the same."

During our return to London, I viewed our countryside investigation in a new light. Small wonder that our unusual driver had considered the matter of the stolen gold with a professional interest. If a smuggler—who must have worked in collusion with some of the local inhabitants at one time—did not know how the stolen gold was removed, then who would?

Chapter 7

~

The Leaden Intruder

THAT EVENING, our dinner at 221 B Baker Street was a quiet one. I was touched by the faith Holmes had evidenced by his revelation on the homebound train and did not wish to plague him with further questions. Many of my queries through the years must have smacked of the inane to him. He frequently displayed irritation when others could not match the mercurial speed of his intellect, but exhibited a singular patience with me. On more than one occasion he had stated that I possessed an intuitive ability to center on a key fact, as though gravitated to the missing piece of a mosaic he was attempting to piece together. His words were sweet music and I invariably glowed when recalling them, but there was the lurking suspicion that he might have strained a point or two in this respect. He invariably referred to *our* investigation and the problems that *we* must solve in a manner so convincing that the words were universally accepted, fortunately for me. Had anyone dared to question Mr. Sherlock Holmes or looked closely at the facade of our equal contributions to case-solving that he had created, they might have burst out laughing. When I allowed my mind to dwell on this, there was the recurring thought that Holmes could have hypnotized himself into actually believing that I was an indispensable cog in the machinery that he had created. An active weapon like Slim Gilligan or, perish the thought, the awesome and frightening Wakefield Orloff.

Holmes seemed preoccupied and, as he so often did when involved in thought, busied himself in his chemical corner. When he was intent on beakers and retorts, conversation was impossible. I decided to bide my time relative to certain matters that still puzzled me about our afternoon expedition. I was attempting, without too much success, to collect and sort notes on a case history that I hoped to make available to my readers, going through the usual exasperation involved in locating certain information and assembling it in the proper order. My friend had a vial full of a dark liquid bubbling furiously. He removed the candle beneath it and placed it on the desk. Holmes was turning back toward his apparatus when the upper pane of one of our bay windows was shattered. There was a booming sound, the candle was abruptly halved, and there was a resounding thud in the far side of the room. I sat transfixed, staring at the reduced candle, convinced that I had felt a disturbance in the air in front of my face, which may or may not have been true. Then I was galvanized into action.

"Holmes, we are being fired upon," I cried, dropping from the desk chair to the floor and making for the window on all fours with the intent of drawing the blind.

"Calm yourself, old fellow," said the sleuth in a casual tone as though asking for a dinner roll.

To my consternation, he made for the door to our chambers with no attempt of concealment.

I lunged back toward him with the half-formed idea of pulling him to the floor so that he would not make such a splendid target, but he was already at our outer portal and had it open.

"Billy," he called, "please inform Mrs. Hudson that naught is amiss. A slight miscalculation in one of my chemical experiments was the cause of the disturbance."

I assumed that the page boy acknowledged this request and made for our landlady's domain. I was, again, scurrying toward the window and had managed to close the drapes by the time Holmes reentered our quarters from the landing.

"Please, Watson, do not be so concerned."

I fear my reply was made with some heat. "Bullets flying through the air and you . . ."

"*A* bullet," he interrupted. "Fired with no intent of doing us harm."

The sleuth retrieved the upper portion of the candle from the floor.

"Remarkable piece of shooting. Had the marksman fired at a human target, one of us would now be dead."

His eyes went upward and, to my horror, he crossed to the window, pulling the blind partially aside to view the shattered pane of glass.

"See the angle of the shot," he said, indicating upward.

"For God's sake, Holmes, close that drape." I had flattened myself against the wall between the windows. "You may be interested in plotting a trajectory, but I'll have no part of your madness."

He did let the material fall back into place and there was concern in his large eyes as he viewed me, frozen in my protected position.

"Good fellow, the crash of a rifle bullet, fired from an elongated barrel I suspect, is a jarring note on a quiet evening at home. Let me repeat that the man behind the gun did not have blood in his eye."

As he spoke he was tracing an imaginary line from the window to the candle, which took him to a point in our floorboards where he squatted, after securing the clasp knife from the mantelpiece.

"Anyone who could sever that candle so neatly could have found either of us with ease had he so wished."

He rose to his feet at this point, displaying a misshapen piece of lead triumphantly.

"I shall inspect this carefully, but other matters claim our attention." He was at the desk now, in the chair I had vacated so precipitously but a short while before, scrawling on foolscap. I could not remain pressed against the wall forever. Drawing a deep breath, I crossed to the settee, casting a nervous glance back at the window through which the whisper of death had entered our sitting room.

"Forgive me if I seem unduly concerned," I began, and there was a liberal touch of irony in my voice.

"Reasonable, of course," he stated with an airy wave of one hand. "Old fellow, the shot was fired from a height. Note the point of entry through the window."

"I'll take your word for it."

"The bullet did not come from across the street or down the block, but from a more distant point. Despite the high-velocity weapon used, the marksman had to allow for a curvature of flight and yet he was able to hit the candle, a slight miscalculation on his part?"

"Miscalculation?" I echoed in an alarmed tone.

"He meant to hit the wick, you see. What a dramatic message that would have been."

"Message? Now see here, Holmes . . ."

"The bullet was just that, Watson, and delivered with more speed and, indeed, impact that a cable or letter. 'See here, Sherlock Holmes, you are but mortal and can be snuffed out as easily as this candle.'"

This gave me pause, for now I understood Holmes's line of thinking. Whilst I mused, the sleuth took the messages he had scrawled and went again to the landing to call Billy. More cables, I thought, and then another idea hit me. There was nothing on my friend's schedule at the moment save the matter of the treasure train. As near as I could figure, we had learned precious little about it up to this point. Yet someone was sufficiently concerned about the investigation to indulge in a striking gesture indeed. I resolved to try and ferret out the missing pieces that Holmes must be privy to but I was not.

Upon his return, I took a stern stand.

"See here, Holmes, I can find no flaw in your reasoning."

"I'm relieved about that," was his dry reply. There was a twinkle in his eyes, but I did not allow it to deter me.

"You must have learned something today and I'm blessed if I can see what it was."

"Because of the warning, you mean. Good thinking."

The sleuth's eyes wandered to the window again and back to the floor from which he had extracted the spent slug.

"We must instigate some repairs, Watson, without Mrs. Hudson's knowledge. If the matter of the shot in the night ever becomes known to the dear woman, I fear her sleep will be disturbed for weeks to come."

"The case, Holmes!" I sputtered with exasperation.

"Ledger showed us the special freight this morning. Did something strike you?"

I shook my head.

"It did me, but then I was looking for corroborative evidence for a theory I had already evolved. Let us accept two basic assumptions and progress from there. First, Ledger was not lying to us. Since we can so easily check his words, it would not seem reasonable for him to fabricate. Therefore, the robbers did not gain access to the train in the freight yards. Two, the guards on the freight were trustworthy. We shall certainly confirm this, but if they were involved in the theft, no mystery exists."

As Holmes secured his clay pipe from the mantel, I muttered that his assumptions seemed, almost certainly, correct.

"All right," he continued. "The robbery occurred during the trip, in the area of the village of Brent. Considering the speed of the freight and the position of the riflemen guarding it, there was no way the thieves could have gotten on the train save from above."

Holmes's careful investigation of the bridge outside of Brent had alerted me to this and I merely nodded.

"A simple arithmetic calculation proves it. We secured the distance from the parapet of the bridge to the top of the freight car."

"You estimated that at twelve feet."

Holmes continued through a cloud of smoke. "Let us assume two men dropped from the bridge to the train top. It was a moving target and they had to land at just the right spot to shove the smoke bombs into the armored cubicle before the guards recovered their wits and started shooting. They couldn't just jump at the spot they hoped to land. They had to lead their target, as the expression goes."

I must have been regarding Holmes blankly, for he explained further.

"Consider the shot just fired through the window, Watson. The marksman didn't aim at the candle, but above it—to allow for the effect of gravity on the bullet. In a similar manner, the train robbers had to anticipate their leap to the moving freight car."

"A moment," I said with a sudden thought. "The white paint on the forward part of the railroad car."

Holmes exhibited that small-boy look of delight that was reserved for those moments when I chimed in with his thinking.

"Exactly. Now we have a formula. The distance they dropped, the rate of descent of a falling object, the speed of the train. I paced off the distance from the paint mark to the rear of the freight car with due consideration for where I thought the robbers landed. My calculations are rough, but I am satisfied that the white line was their signal to leap from the bridge."

"You were looking for something like that since you'd already decided that they had come from above." I made haste to add what was for me a rather inspired bit of reasoning. "Ofttimes you have noted that whenever all else proves impossible, what remains must be true. They had to come from above, no other direction being possible."

"Watson, you never fail to amaze me." He was joshing, of course, but I was so enthused that I did not let it faze me until a second thought cast doubts, as second thoughts so often do.

"Your recreation is up to your highest standards, Holmes, but dashed if I see where it has been revealing."

"Don't you? Give it a try, old fellow."

I certainly did and suddenly, somewhat to my surprise, a thought struck me.

"Why, of course. Whoever robbed the train had to have access to the freight cars well in advance."

"Right, Watson. Ledger said that Alvidon Chasseur was responsible for the paint mark and, in the rush, it was not completely removed. I inspected it rather closely and don't choose to agree with him."

"One moment," I exclaimed, trying to sort out my mixed up thoughts. "Chasseur had a rectangle painted as a guide to the construction of the armored cubicle . . . then it was decided to alter its position and the mark was partially painted out."

"That's what Ledger said. However, I scraped off some of the white paint. I think the marking was completely painted out."

"Then someone renewed that particular portion to serve as an eye marker for the robbers," I said breathlessly.

My friend nodded. "Again we have evidence of meticulous planning. However, I dwell on the obvious. The robbery succeeded, which speaks well for the ingenuity of its architect if not for his moral code."

Holmes rose from his armchair and walked toward the windows, his chin on his chest. He must have noted my instinctive reaction of alarm, for he reversed his direction and paced in a circle around the center of the room. He had once told me that a coffin would make a superior place to lie in silence and solitude and wrestle with a problem. That was but his mood of the moment, for I knew that many times he liked to think on his feet.

Events did not allow him to wear a furrow in our carpet as he pondered, nor did I expect them to. My friend, no doubt to calm my panic, had made light of our leaden intruder that had come at us from the darkness of the night, but I knew he took it as a personal affront. The thought of counterattack had to be in his mind and I was not surprised when there was the sound of footsteps on the seventeen steps leading to the landing and Billy ushered in the wise-eyed Slim Gilligan, select member of what I chose to call the inside group.

A cloth cap was at a jaunty angle on his head, and an unlit cigarette was tucked behind one ear. A heavy black sweater served as his coat, no surprise since Slim eschewed clothing of a bulky nature because getting in and out of places was his greatest talent. His attire always had a streamlined look, devoid of anything that might catch on a projection or slow him down. His movements had an oily grace and he never seemed rushed, though I knew of only one man who could, when necessary, move faster and that man was not Holmes.

"Evenin', guv. What's on the slate tonight?"

Holmes gestured toward the particles of glass still on the rug by the window. Slim's lips pursed for a brief moment. From him, that was akin to a broad gesture of astonishment from someone else. He cat-footed his way to the window, peering at the shattered pane briefly from the side of the drape as though he knew what he'd find. When he turned back, there was a tightening of his jaw muscles.

"Fired from a distance. Judging from the shards of glass, a smallish bullet, I'd say."

Holmes retrieved the lead slug from the desktop

and tossed it to the cracksman, whose unusually long hand swallowed it in midair. He stood turning the lead pellet between his talented fingers for a moment. "Not my line, guv, but I'd say it's foreign make."

"Mauser is my guess," replied Holmes. Those were the first words he'd spoken since the former safe cracker had entered the room. With Slim, Holmes seldom had to explain much.

The man's large brown eyes were now on me. "Glad to see you is tip-top, Doc." His jaunty smile was momentary and from habit. His features had a grim quality as he regarded my friend again.

"We can't 'ave this, you know." It was the first time I had actually seen Gilligan angry and one had to look closely to come to that conclusion. He seemed to consider the shot fired at the sacred confines of our dwelling as a personal insult.

"It was a warning, Slim, relative to a matter I'm now involved in," said Holmes soothingly.

Gilligan's manner remained hostile toward persons unknown. "I know you got some ideas, Mr. 'Olmes, but why don't you let Slim take a pass at this?"

Oh dear, I thought, if Holmes allows his number one lieutenant in the underworld to go unchecked, Limehouse and Soho are due for an uncomfortable time.

"Let's play a different tune, Slim," said the sleuth. "I'll not tolerate Mrs. Hudson or Billy being placed in jeopardy, so Bertie and Tiny are on their way here now."

The muscles in Gilligan's jaw relaxed. The great detective's remark was not the non sequitur it might seem at first glance. He never displayed the slightest concern about his personal safety, but any thought of harm befalling our kindly landlady or loyal page boy filled him with alarm.

Holmes continued. "You might have a word with the boys about what to do and arrange a backup for them."

Gilligan nodded, and I knew the reason for the sudden humor in his eyes. With Burlington Bertie and his brother Tiny on the job, the Coldstream Guards would have a difficult time forcing their way into our domicile.

"Then," said Holmes, "you could take a look around, Slim. It rather had to be a rooftop. The bird has long since flown, but there might be something to find."

"I'll know where to look, guv," was the cracksman's brief reply.

"We want our ears to the ground, and the whisper is gold. Half a million pounds' worth."

Gilligan nodded. "The bullion heist. There's naught in the streets 'bout it save a lot of envious boyos who's wishin' they'd pulled the caper."

"See what you can learn. We'll use the usual contact."

"Righto, guv. Rest easy. Slim's on ta job."

Gilligan was gone. The imagination plays one tricks and mine was stimulated by Slim's reputation as the greatest cracksman of his day, but he never seemed to arrive and depart like normal folk. Rather, he materialized and then vanished in true genie fasion. Whatever his peculiarities, I knew I could enjoy a night's rest without worry. Slim and the boys from Limehouse would throw a net around 221 B Baker Street. Even as exacting a tactician as our former client General Sternways would have been forced to concede that the command post was secure.

Chapter 8

❧

A Message from Shadrach

THE FOLLOWING morning I descended to our sitting room somewhat earlier than usual, spurred no doubt by the new problem that faced the master man hunter. I had left my friend the night before musing while writing cables that would be sent via Billy the page boy. I doubted that the sleuth had spent the entire night on the matter at hand since, at this point, he had so little to work with.

Holmes was absent, which meant that he had breakfasted early and gone about certain investigations that he wished to pursue alone. Mrs. Hudson informed me that he had left no message, so I decided to brave the outside world myself, there being some matters relative to my practice that required attention.

Visits to the offices of Vernier and Goodbody resulted in certain patient calls that involved more time than I had anticipated. Darkness had fallen when I returned to 221 B Baker Street. A storm was brewing over the great city. Low scud clouds, like celestial dragon boats of ghostly Viking raiders, sailed majestically overhead. Riding in the teeth of a high wind that blew from the direction of Scapa Flow, they were pounderously bypassing London to, no doubt, disgorge their contents on the Cornish coast and Lands End. The air was thick with moisture and I assumed the great metropolis was due for a washing down before the night was over. As I climbed to the door of our first-floor sitting room, it crossed my mind that it was a splendid night to sit by the fire and work on a recent bit of research. It related to the possibility of genetic information being passed from one generation to the next. While the idea had come to me relative to a participant in the Sacred Sword matter, I had clung to it as a possible explanation for some of the amazing abilities of Sherlock Holmes.

When I opened our hall door, I found the fire crackling merrily in the hearth. Holmes was seated at the desk, blowing smoke rings at the ceiling.

"Ah, Watson, you precede the rain to our chambers."

"Good thing, too," I muttered, placing my medical bag beside the cane rack and shrugging myself out of my greatcoat. "The night gives every indication of being a rouser."

"A good time to be within." Holmes indicated a cable open on the desk. "Especially with material on hand to feed that ravenous mechanism called the mind."

"*Quid novi?*" I asked, making for the bottles on our sideboard.

Holmes's eyebrows elevated at my root language query.

"The news is considerable," he replied. "With our lines in the water, some pedestrian investigation was called for, hence my early departure this morning. I've interviewed two of the railroad guards on the bullion train. Their statements confirmed our thoughts on the matter. They both recall sounds that alerted them."

"The robbers alighting on the boxcar roof."

"Exactly. But before they could make note of anything, the smoke bombs were inside their vantage point and their recollections ceased to be of any use."

"Could the smoke have had a narcotic effect?" I asked suddenly.

Holmes shook his head. "Doubtful. Last night I was attempting to discover what chemical combination might have been used. To no avail, I might add."

"Something else happened then, for you seem well pleased."

"Have I become obvious through the years?" The sleuth indicated the cable I had noted. "A considerable report from our friend John Bennett, constable of Shaw, on the late Ezariah Trelawney."

"*Quid pro quo*," I said without meaning to.

"My, you are of a scholarly turn this evening," commented Holmes. "A working arrangement between elements of law and order is beneficial, as I'm sure you agree. Bennett has unearthed interesting possibilites." He indicated the letter again. "I'm trying to decipher *quid hoc sibi vult*." There was a twinkle in his eye and I wished that I had never resorted to the few scraps of Latin patient instructors had pounded into me.

"What does that mean?" I asked registering defeat.

" 'What does *this* mean' is the exact translation, old chap. Bennett's report might mean a lot. When we investigated the death of Ezariah Trelawney, all we knew about his background was his trade, banking."

"Along with the blood feud that played such an important part in the matter."

"Agreed. You do recall that Trelawney's association with the bullion matter decided me on accepting the case?"

"I've wondered about that."

Holmes took a cigarette from the desk container. "I am too much of a pragmatist to dwell on thoughts of a predetermined destiny. However, ofttimes fate does enter the picture and I chose to follow its beckoning finger this time."

I placed a whiskey and water on the desk for Holmes and retreated with my own to the armchair beside the fire, my brain awhirl. Despite our long association, I had seldom been able to anticipate his unerring logic, but the years had made me conscious of certain signposts that occasionally pointed me down the right path.

"You think that Trelawney's death is tied up with the bullion matter." I took a sip and then rejected this idea. "But we solved the banker's murder."

"Did we?" questioned Holmes. "We discovered that Vincent Staley attempted to plant the Trelawney murder weapon on Horace Ledbetter. He then attacked Ledbetter and was killed by him. Because of the circumstances, we assumed Staley killed the banker, but that fact was never proven."

"I doubt if it can be now."

"I'm forced to agree with that, Watson. However, Ezariah Trelawney was involved in the shipment of gold to the Credit Lyonnais, so I had Constable Bennett instigate additional inquiries. Trelawney was miserly. As a young man he was with the army in the Crimea." Suddenly the sleuth's keen gaze shifted to the door. Then I heard footfalls on the landing.

"Come in, Billy," said Holmes as there was a gentle knock.

" 'Tis Inspector MacDonald, sir," said the page boy from the half-open door.

"Show him up, by all means," replied the detective.

I was amazed at this turn of events. The anticipated storm had broken while Holmes and I had talked and the wind was blowing at near gale proportions. Wailing gusts served as an eerie chorus for the timpani of rain spattering against the glass of our Baker Street windows.

It was a wet and disheveled Inspector Alec MacDonald who entered our sitting room. As I helped him out of his coat, Holmes stirred up the hearth fire so that it radiated a welcome warmth for the dour Scot. A comfortable chair and an extra tumbler from the sideboard erased MacDonald's scowl, but there was still considerable dissatisfaction on his rough hewn face as he toasted us both and took a sizeable draft.

Holmes's eyes twinkled as he regarded our visitor.

"If we've driven the chill from your bones, old fellow, possibly we can also relieve your inner stress. It is obvious your coming tonight was no idle whim. A troublesome case, perhaps?"

"I wish I was sure," replied the inspector. " 'Tis the matter of Ramsey Michael."

At the sideboard, replenishing my drink, I heard Holmes's glass come in contact with the desktop forcibly. As I turned at this unusual sound, I found the sleuth regarding MacDonald intently.

"The so-called art critic," said the sleuth. "What problem involves him?"

"Ah then, you haven't heard. He was shot to death this very evening."

"Good heavens!" I exclaimed involuntarily, though I did not know the man referred to.

Something was bothering Holmes, but his laconic comment was unrevealing.

"The gentleman was not popular. Do we face one of those cases devoid of clues?"

"Few needed," said MacDonald somewhat bitterly. "We have one suspect and what looks like an airtight case. And yet there's something about it that doesn't sit comfortable." He glanced at me shamefaced, then centered on Holmes again. "You'll make sport of me for saying it, but the taste isn't right."

Holmes was gazing at the inspector with added respect. "After a lengthy career in the field of criminology, it would be strange indeed if you did not possess a distinct feel for such matters. My congratulations, Mr. Mac. Now do tell us of the affair and what specifically wrinkles your nose with doubt."

MacDonald had a wary look, as if suspecting that he was being twitted, but the great consulting detective was completely serious so the Aberdonian plunged into his tale.

"Michael's body was found by his butler at six this evening in the upstairs study of his home on Belgrave Square. A bullet from an Adams .450 revolver caught him right between the eyes and was lodged in his brain. Death was instantaneous."

"You established the make and caliber of the murder weapon with admirable promptness," commented Holmes.

"And without difficulty, since the gun was on the floor of the room." MacDonald exhibited a sly smile. "Before you ask, we did check the weapon for fingerprints, and there were none."

"None at all, or none that could be identified?"

"The gun had been wiped clean." At a nod from Holmes, the inspector continued. "Besides Michael, there were three other occupants of the house. Herndon, the butler, and his wife, Matilda, who is cook-housekeeper. Also a Miss Vanessa Claremont, who was Michael's ward."

"Something was nagging at me and now I have it," I ventured. "Miss Claremont is a patient of Dr. Vernier. He has spoken to me of her." Inasmuch as the inspector and Holmes were regarding me with considerable interest, I continued.

"Miss Claremont is but twenty-three and suffers from pernicious anemia. Vernier has her on a special diet fortified with liver, but the case bothers him. She weighs but seven stone and is a frail reed indeed."

MacDonald had a sour look about his mouth. "I'm told that Michael did not treat the poor thing at all well. Perhaps that has colored my thinking. But let me conclude this strange tale," he said with a sigh.

"Michael was not outside his house the entire day. The mansion itself has a bearing on the case. It contains art objects of considerable value and is something of a fortress. Bars on all the windows and secure locks on stout doors. It was the habit of the household to make sure everything was bolted up come nightfall."

"Shortly after five this time of year." Holmes's eyes were dreamy with thought.

MacDonald nodded in agreement. "It was the sound of the firearm that alarmed the butler, Herndon. He came from the servants' quarters on the run to find Vanessa Claremont on the stairs leading to the upstairs study. She said that she had been in her ground floor quarters when she heard the shot and had started up instinctively but had become frightened."

"Whereas she might well have fired the gun and started down, for all the butler knew," suggested Holmes.

"Indeed, sir. In any case, Herndon discovered the body and raced downstairs to summon a constable. Rushing by Miss Claremont, he shouted that the master was dead, at which point she fainted. Fortunately there was an officer close-by on the Square and he returned with the butler. Herndon and his wife revived Miss Claremont while the constable notified the Yard and there you are."

The inspector leaned back in his chair as if relieved to have gotten the main narrative out of the way. He knew that pertinent questions would be asked.

Holmes was regarding the dancing flames in the hearth fire thoughtfully.

"You said there was but one suspect and a seemingly airtight case. Let me see. The house was securely locked about an hour before the fatal shot. I assume that is confirmed by direct testimony?"

MacDonald nodded. "As was the custom, Herndon checked all the doors and windows shortly after five. Miss Claremont confirms this, since she was cleaning downstairs at the time." Since Holmes made no comment, the inspector continued. "Actually, Miss Claremont was little better than a maid in the establishment. She is the niece of Michael's deceased wife, and the art critic took her in because of a proviso in Mrs. Michael's will. But he did not relish the arrangement and made no effort to conceal his feelings."

"No love lost between the two." Holmes resumed his musings. "I assume the shot that alerted the household was the one that killed Michael."

"We had a pathologist on the scene in short order," replied the inspector. "Just as a matter of procedure, since the corpse was still bleeding when the constable got there. He was shot at six for a fact."

"Your prime suspect is obviously the ward, Vanessa Claremont," stated Holmes. "Motive must point the finger of guilt."

"Indeed, sir. Neither Herndon, the butler, nor his wife had reason to wish their master dead. On the other hand, Miss Claremont stands to inherit Michael's estate. If she evades the gallows for his murder, that is." The Scot was shaking his head.

"Miss Claremont had both motive and opportunity. You are still dissatisfied?"

"Aye, sir. 'Tis the feel."

"I agree completely," was Sherlock Holmes's surprising response.

I rose from my chair with a groan. "So it's off to the scene of the crime, is it? I could wish murders would occur during more clement weather."

My confrere chuckled. "Do resume your seat, old fellow, unless you wish to replenish Mr. Mac's glass. I have no intention of going forth on this night. We shall consider the problem in comfortable surroundings."

"Will you, now?" MacDonald seemed ruffled, but his manner mellowed when I forced a refill on him along with a cigar.

"More questions, of course," stated Holmes. "Ramsey Michael went through the motions of being a busy man and he did not stray from his domicile during the day. I assume there were visitors?"

"Three." The inspector referred to his official notebook. "At one in the afternoon Mr. Ezra Hinshaw consulted with Michael about a lecture at the

Tate Museum. He transacted his business rapidly and left in short order. At three, a Vicar Bisbee arrived in hopes of securing a donation for a local charity. Whether Michael complied or not I haven't learned, but the vicar is well known in those parts. He is somewhat deaf and quite nearsighted."

"We can rule out Bisbee for obvious reasons," remarked Holmes.

Aside from the vicar's line of work, I could divine no obvious reasons but withheld comment on the matter.

"Around four-thirty, one Cedric Folks visited Michael. Bit of a neer-do-well, that one. Orbits 'round the edge of society as a painter of sorts. Attended Sandhurst but left under something of a cloud. Haven't run him down yet but evidently his visit to Michael was connected with the art world. Folks was not expected at the establishment and Herndon was reluctant to admit him. Folks asked the butler to tell his master that he brought a message from Shadrach."

"Now that's interesting," said Holmes. "Sounds a bit like a code. I assume Michael agreed to see the fellow?"

"He instructed the butler to show Folks up to his first-story study. The artist left shortly before five, slamming the front door forceably. This sound brought the butler into the hall. Michael appeared at the head of the stairs and directed the servant to secure the doors carefully. Herndon told me that Michael appeared angry. It was the last time he saw the art critic alive."

"Did the butler make any other comment about this incident?"

MacDonald's brow furrowed in thought. "Simply that he went through his regular procedure of shooting the bolts on the front door and then checking the windows. Wait a wee bit," the inspector added. "He did say he heard horses' hooves outside and saw Folks's hansom depart."

Holmes rubbed his hands with satisfaction. "Now, as the butler went about his regular task, Michael returned to his upstairs study I assume?"

"Yes, sir. As the butler completed his security tour, Miss Claremont went to her room on the ground floor. She engaged in needlework, but her door was open. She stated that neither Herndon nor his wife came from the servant quarters before the shot was fired. Because of the layout of the house, they would have had to pass her door."

I was intrigued by this. "The prime suspect gives the servants a foolproof alibi. She might better have kept silent on the matter."

"Incontestable alibis arouse my suspicions," remarked Holmes. "But it is no matter since I have learned what I wish to know. Gentlemen, a prima facie case for your consideration."

The very manner in which he leaned back in his chair told the story. The calm theorist of Baker Street was ready with another tour de force.

"Daily study of the journals makes one privy to seemingly odd incidents which prove helpful in solving puzzles. Cedric Folks is attempting a career in art and had a showing recently. In covering the event, Michael stated in print that the painter was obviously trying to emulate the French Impressionist Pissarro, but that his paintings created naught but a false impression. This acid critique elicited much ribald laughter in art circles, and Folks, I must assume, became livid with rage. Recall his stormy departure from the presence of the art critic. You did mention that he slammed the outer door loudly."

The Scot, his eyes intent on Holmes, nodded briefly.

"Now, Mr. Mac, regarding the upstairs study where Michael met his end. It is sizeable?"

"More than thirty feet in length."

"And the door to the study is adjacent to the staircase?"

"How did you know that?"

"To fit my reconstruction, it had to be."

I thought my friend's smile was somewhat smug but quelled the thought, being on tenterhooks for the denouement.

Holmes resumed his summation. "Three members of the household, not counting the corpse, and three visitors during the day. The man from the museum and the vicar can be ruled out, surely, for complete lack of motive, not to mention means. But Cedric Folks, the irate artist, had motive. Of the others, the servants are given an alibi by Vanessa Claremont. She had motive. They did not. Miss Claremont has an alibi."

"If she does, I canna' see it."

"Come now! A frail young woman shoots Michael with a .450 Adams revolver? I doubt she could even manage the trigger pull of such a heavy caliber weapon. But to expect her to fire it with the accuracy of a marksman over a distance of thirty feet is asking the impossible."

"Could she not have been close to Michael when she shot him?" MacDonald was far from convinced.

"Had Miss Claremont been near the victim, the bullet would have torn through his head. You said it was lodged in his brain. Come, come, Inspector; we are speaking of a heavy piece of ordinance with high muzzle velocity."

MacDonald shot me a sheepish look. "He's right, you know," was his grudging admission.

"He usually is," I replied.

"I ruled out your prime suspect promptly," continued Holmes. "When Cedric Folks rushed down the stairs shortly before five, he opened the front door and then slammed it shut without his leaving the house. Instead, he concealed himself within. Behind a convenient sofa, perhaps. The butler, thinking he had left, locked up the house. Outside there was the sound of the departing hansom. When the time seemed right, Folks stole up the stairs, opened the door to the study and, as Michael turned at the sound, he fired from the doorway. He did attend Sandhurst, you said. I'll wager you will learn that he is an excellent shot. Wiping the gun clean, he threw it into the murder room and raced down the stairs to hide below. The body was discovered, the butler rushed outside, and Miss Claremont fainted. At this point, Folks escaped from the house unnoticed, though he might have done so later, when the constable arrived and all attention was directed to the first-floor study, where the victim's body lay. There's your case for you, MacDonald, all tied up neatly." The detective directed a smile at me. "And the resolution did not require Watson's braving the elements after all."

The inspector was shaking his head. "I've a thought that I'm going to look like a fool, but there's one wee matter, Mr. Holmes. If Folks did not leave the house around five, how was it that the hansom that brought him departed?"

"But that's the whole key to the matter. I can reconstruct what happened but how can you prove it in court? Folks hired the cab and instructed its driver to leave when he slammed the front door. He gave the man a sizeable fee, no doubt. The hansom driver is the tool to force a confession from Folks. Just locate him and you have your witness to the fact that the artist did not leave the Michael mansion at five o'clock."

At last MacDonald seemed satisfied. "That artist fellow will learn that it doesn't pay to have a temper that matches his hair."

Holmes's self-satisfied expression vanished. "Let us run that last statement by again, Mr. Mac. You imply that Folks is redheaded?"

"You don't know him?"

"Never set eyes on the fellow."

"Well I suspect there's some Irish in his background, for he is a carrot top and that's a fact."

MacDonald had risen from his chair and I helped him on with his topcoat. "You've tied him up in a knot, Mr. Holmes, and I'm grateful," continued the Scot, his normally dour expression erased by grim satisfaction.

Holmes did not share his enthusiasm. "The third caller at the Michael mansion is your murderer, Mr. Mac, but his identity is still to be proven."

"Come now, Mr. Holmes. You always were one for dotting the *i*'s and crossing the *t*'s but I've got my man, thanks to you."

Holmes shrugged. "Cedric Folks will certainly have to be questioned, but if there is any problem relative to him, we shall speak again on the matter."

It was after Inspector MacDonald left that Holmes turned toward me with a lazy smile.

"At first glance, this matter seemed bizarre indeed. An *outré* affair. But it was all quite simple, really."

Surely his words wrote *finis* to the matter, but his manner did not.

"Please don't say *elementary*," I replied. "You surely solved MacDonald's problem, and mine as well since our departure into the night was not necessary at all."

"In a short while MacDonald may not be as satisfied with the resolution of the Michael death as he is right now. However, we did exonerate Miss Vanessa Claremont, which was the matter of immediate importance. The so-called Cedric Folks is a sticky wicket, I fear."

"You say so-called?" My query was automatic, for this had to be the fly in Holmes's ointment.

"A redheaded man presented himself at the Michael abode and called himself Cedric Folks. I have doubts about his being the irate painter."

"But why? Folks had a motive for wishing to do Michael in."

"Agreed. Injured pride and rage, fueled by an artistic temperament, can cause feelings to run high, but not often to the white heat required for murder. Then we have the matter of Trelawney to consider."

"Surely there is no connection."

"Possibly not. However young Charles Trelawney was the prime suspect because the stationmaster at Shaw saw him get off the six o'clock special. He testified, as I recall, that there were but two arrivals. Charles and a redheaded stranger."

"Dear me," I mouthed with a frown. "I'd quite forgotten about that. Do you think the same redheaded man . . ."

Holmes rose briskly to his feet and began pacing the length of our sitting room.

"Let us not jump to assumptions, but just consider this as a possibility. We have two murders, with a redheaded man on the scene of both. Not necessarily the same person, but it does give one pause. One way to disguise identity is to alter one's appearance, presenting to the unobservant eye an inconspicuous and false figure. Another is to adopt a striking characteristic."

"Like red hair," I cried suddenly. "You envision an assassin using a wig so that anyone noting his presence would identify him as being redheaded. Which, of course, he is not," I added, and was rather pleased with my understanding of Holmes's idea.

"We are in agreement on that last point," said the sleuth, returning to his favorite chair beside the fire.

"But wait, Holmes, are you not running far afield? Could not the banker Trelawney have been killed by Horace Ledbetter? Mightn't Michael have been shot by the real Cedric Folks in the manner you outlined to MacDonald?"

"Agreed on both points," replied Holmes with a prompt acceptance that made me suspicious.

"Yet something got your hackles up," I continued. "Some clue perhaps?" My voice dwindled away as I racked my brains to no avail.

There was a mischievous twinkle in Holmes's sharp eyes. "The third caller on the departed Michael made a singular statement to the butler, Herndon."

"A message from Shadrach?" I said, dredging words from my memory. "You suggested a code."

"Sounds like one." Holmes's relaxed thoughtful mood vanished and his expression sharpened. "But I have played you false, good fellow. I do have certain information that you are not privy to. Evidently MacDonald as well, since he made no mention of it."

Holmes was gazing into the fireplace. A silence fell between us which I did not break, knowing well that he was considering a theory.

Finally he spoke and I imagined a trace of

approval in his tone, as though his analysis had withstood the tests he placed upon it.

"Ramsey Michael on several occasions has flitted on the periphery of investigations that came our way. There was the Bishopegate Jewel Case, for one.* But no matter. The point is that he maintained a considerable establishment, was able to gather a collection of costly objects, and enjoyed a certain reputation as an art critic, an occupation not noteworthy for its direct remuneration."

"You suspect that he had a concealed source of income?"

"Especially since I took the trouble to establish that he was not blessed with inherited wealth. Michael could well have been a member of a small and clandestine group known as expediters."

Holmes shot a quick glance at me but received a blank stare for his trouble, so he continued.

"A necessary strut in the framework of illegal activities. A man who can grease the machinery and, on occasion, set up a certain situation."

"A go-between. As, for instance, one who arranges for the disposition of stolen property. Sometimes before the theft is committed," I added, my mind going back to the Bishopegate case and how Holmes had lectured the force upon it.

"Stout fellow," said Holmes approvingly.

"But now new vistas beckon," I stated with some excitement. "If Ramsey Michael had a shadowy background, his murder could well have stemmed from it. You did rather hold out on MacDonald, Holmes."

"Not at all," was his swift reply. "The matter of Cedric Folks has to be explored. If the former soldier turned artist is indeed the culprit, my thought does not pass muster."

---

*Spelling used by Watson. Was there another Bishopgate case?

Holmes seemed about to continue and then his lips compressed in a thin line and his eyes reverted to the fireplace, taking on an opaque look they sometimes did when his mind was churning with a new thought.

"That is an interesting statement I just made," he continued after a moment.

Of a sudden, I felt in tune with his thinking.

"Ledger is a former soldier," I exclaimed.

"So was Trelawney," said the sleuth, as though talking to himself. "Though of much older vintage. It crosses my mind that the late Ramsey Michael was reputed to have served in the Crimea as well."

"Ah hah. You have established a possible connection between Michael and Ezariah Trelawney."

Holmes's predatory features swiveled in my direction. "Michael and Ezariah, you say, Watson? Not for the first time, you have come up with a seemingly commonplace remark that suggests fascinating overtones."

I was pleased to have been of help but completely at sea as to what he was thinking of.

"Shadrach," he murmured in a tone so soft that I was pressed to distinguish the single word.

Then Holmes was out of his chair making for the bookcase.

"Research is called for, old fellow, and we have an excellent file on the train robbery as well as the material Mycroft so kindly placed at our disposal."

Holmes took the *M* volume from the row of file volumes and had the wick of the desk lamp raised in but a moment. I assumed the late Ramsey Michael had first call on his attention and I noted that the material he had received from his brother was already on the desk surface.

Suddenly I ceased to exist as far as my intimate friend was concerned. He was leafing through pages and, from experience, I knew he would be referring to his commonplace book before too long. The walls of our familiar habitat and the intimates within had faded into a nothingness for Holmes, who, with rapid steps, was traversing the wonderland of his mental world and completely absorbed in his journey.

His abrupt preoccupation, not uncommon during our years together, was irritating nonetheless. But a moment before we had been discussing possibilities in a case that was certainly producing added complexities. Now I was shunted off, discarded, and this produced annoyance that led to a testy remark as I prepared to make my way upstairs to my waiting bed.

"I am reminded, Holmes, of your frequent cautionary statements about the premature acceptance of a theory. Do you not contend that it risks the adjusting of facts to fit it?"

My words produced no reaction from Holmes whatsoever. I had risen from my chair and extinguished my cigar before his noble head rose and he turned toward me.

"Good, loyal, Watson. I can only say, *touché*, old comrade. However, do recall that I have a kind of intuition based on special knowledge gathered through the years. But your warning does not go unrecorded."

I must say I felt considerably better as I made my way up the backstairs toward the waiting arms of Morpheus.

Chapter 9

❧

To Fenley in Gloucester

I⊤ WAS somewhat late the following morning when I literally staggered down to our sitting room and alerted Mrs. Hudson to my needs. The great silver coffee urn was suitably hot, and I made free of its contents in an effort to dissipate my torpid condition. When I heard Holmes's footfalls on the stairs outside, I shook my head vigorously in an effort to deny the lassitude that plagued me. Keeping up with the mercurial mind of my intimate friend was a losing game for my plodding intellect. This particular morning I felt as though the task would prove insurmountable.

To my disgust, Holmes came through our outer door in a smart tweed suit looking for all the world like he had slept the clock around. I knew it was quite possible that he had not been to bed at all, since one could never tell by his appearance. Especially when he felt the need to bustle about and view things with his own eyes. Surely he was nearing the zenith of his career and his sources of information were enormous. But, as in those early days when he was making his name known throughout the civilized world, nothing pleased him more than to be on the move and doing things directly. With a cheery good morning, he hung his Inverness on a peg behind our door and deposited his tweed flapped cap in a convenient chair.

"Delighted to see that you are with us, old fellow. The early morning has proven profitable and we'd best get to Liverpool Station straight away. If you care to pursue this matter further with me?" he added quickly.

His final remark had been so much twaddle as I well knew and Holmes knew I knew it. The thought of my abandoning a matter involving the robbery of the treasure train and possibly two murders as well was inconceivable.

"Where are we off to?" I asked, disposing of a final rasher of bacon.

"The city of Fenley," he responded. "You do recall that certain west coast banks were involved with the missing gold shipment."

"Then the matter of Ramsey Michael is abandoned?"

"Scotland Yard, in the person of MacDonald, can follow up on that for the moment. The half-million pounds' worth of gold is our principal concern."

I became somewhat nettled and posed my next question more abruptly than usual.

"All right. What in Gloucester relates to the gold shipment?"

"Burton Hananish, financier, lives there."

"The name means nothing to me."

"It would had you gone through the dossier Mycroft placed at our disposal. Hananish was instrumental in creating the cartel that gathered the gold. He has had considerable dealings in the international world of finance. The original idea of the loan to the Credit Lyonnais might have been his."

"I thought Ezariah Trelawney was the key man there."

"Actually, I rather fancy another man completely."

"Michael? The idea man."

"Correct, old fellow," he said, accepting the cup of coffee I had poured for him. A few moments with Holmes and my morning fogginess had evaporated.

I had a sudden thought. "A number of bankers must have been involved. What made you settle on this Hananish chap?"

"He's the only one who is a veteran of the Crimea campaign."

That was all I could get out of Holmes for a while.

Fenley was a modest-sized city in Gloucester, north of Bristol on the Severn River. We were able to travel a through train of the Bristol and Western Railroad, a convenience on our considerable journey. During the trip, Holmes seemed intent on avoiding discussion of the matter that took us toward the west coast. Rather, he spent a lengthy period of time with his long legs stretched out in our first-class compartment, his chin on his chest and his hat lowered over his forehead. I could not tell whether his eyes were closed or not. He might have been sleeping or possibly idly regarding the toes of his shoes with his mind elsewhere. We were approaching Swindon when he roused himself and relieved my boredom with reminiscences regarding the matter of the Netherlands-Sumatra Company and the colossal schemes of Baron Maupertuis. I thought at first that the sleuth was merely whiling away the time in a manner calculated to keep me from posing insane questions. But then the thought of the involvement of the Credit Lyonnais in the Netherlands-Sumatra scandal came to mind. Holmes contended that there was a strong family resemblance about misdeeds. Certainly his knowledge of the history of crime was unequaled, for he had the details of a thousand cases at his fingertips. Was there something in common between the Netherlands-Sumatra matter and the stolen gold? I listened with added attention to his recapitulation and even posed some questions relative to points still unclear in my mind. Since I hope to present a complete account of this matter in a future publication, I shall not dwell further on our discussion, which lasted until our arrival in Fenley.

On descending from our train in the small Gloucester town, I anticipated that we would locate Burton Hananish, the man who had captured Holmes's attention, but this was not the case. We made for the local inn, but a block from the railroad station on a pleasant tree-lined street. It was called the Red Grouse and I judged the management had held tenure for some time and was of a diligent nature. The spigots in the barroom and the rail as well were highly polished while the plank flooring had that sheen that came from oil applied with muscle grease. There was the not unpleasant aroma of malted liquids and a fair sprinkling of customers at the bar consuming same. Holmes not only unerringly walked to the establishment but, without pause, led me to a table in the place that was already occupied. This did not surprise me. My friend had spent a considerable part of the previous twenty-four hours involved in his own pursuits and I suspected that he had established a liaison in Fenley, for he seemed capable of reaching people in almost every locale. We were greeted by a youngish chap, faultlessly dressed, with a low-keyed though hearty voice.

"Gentlemen," he said, indicating the two vacant chairs available.

"Watson, this is Wally," said Sherlock Holmes.

As I took the proffered seat, I reflected that our greetings were both limited and unusual. Holmes did not refer to people by their first names, but he did not choose to elaborate. Wally evidently knew of us both, though his face was not familiar to me. His hair was sandy and cut short and his cheeks glowed from a very close shave. There was an aroma of toilet water about him and I judged it to be expensive. He was close to six feet, slim, and certainly would be judged handsome by the fairer sex. His manner was even more pleasing. I realized that while we had just met and barely that, there was a feeling that we were on the threshold of a pleasant association. I could not explain this aura other than that it emanated from Wally like the after-shave I had noted.

There were no preambles to the conversation, and it took no genius to realize that the youngish fellow was present for a purpose with which he was already well acquainted. I got the feeling that Wally and the sleuth did not know each other, though their words did not indicate this.

"How goes it?" asked Holmes.

"Up and up so far, Mr. Holmes. The man in question has a reputation that you might call . . . like Gibraltar." His searching for a phrase jogged me into the realization that his speech pattern was non-revealing. He sounded like a university man, though I could not guess which one and, indeed, would have been hard pressed to figure out his point of origin. I assumed he was British, but there was no revealing patois or accent.

"Hananish has an international reputation as

well," said Holmes. "I'm rather interested in that aspect of his career."

The barman appeared at this moment and we all ordered stout.

"It is a mite early in the game," continued Holmes, "but do you anticipate problems?"

"No, sir," replied Wally. "With the assistance you've made available, I can get a surface check in a short while. As to how deep I can dig . . ." He let a shrug complete his sentence.

"It would be better if I had something specific for you to look for," said the sleuth. "Perhaps I can come up with something."

"You're going to see him?"

Holmes nodded.

"He's got a rather spiffy estate on the river road. Bit of the local baronet, though without title."

"I know," said Holmes. "Have we learned anything particular about him? Personal life, I mean."

"His raft of servants seem to walk in dread of the old boy. There's a similar feeling among his bank employees, I judge. Cripple, you know."

"I didn't," admitted Holmes.

"Riding accident some time back. He's limited to a wheelchair, which is handled by a brute of a fellow of local origin who is a mute."

"Little to be learned from him." There was a period of silence and then Holmes shoved his half-consumed tankard to one side. "We will use the regular contact, and if that is not convenient, the post office will do. Sorry to have to put you on to this with such short notice."

"Yours to command, Mr. Holmes. I'm much convenienced by your associate being on the scene."

I thought this was a very sporty remark for Wally to make and wondered how I was of assistance to him. It was when we left the barroom of the Red

Grouse that it occurred to me that I might not be the associate the young man referred to.

Holmes secured a carriage near the depot and we traveled but a short distance down the river road to the home of Burton Hananish. It was an Elizabethan mansion and as we drew up in front of the hall door, I noted the gleaming waters of the Severn on our right. Our coming had been observed and servants were already waiting. No doubt one of Holmes's innumerable cables had been sent to the establishment, which was obviously forewarned of our arrival.

A staid and proper butler greeted us at the main entry and accepted Holmes's card, though he scarcely glanced at it. Securing our outer apparel, he led us to a spacious and lofty room and the presence of his master.

Perhaps it was my imagination but there seemed to be an unusual silence about the place, as though everyone walked on tiptoe and in fear and trembling. Certainly Hananish, seated in the wheelchair we had been told of, was not an awe-inspiring figure. His aquiline face was kindly, nay quite beautiful, though touched by the inevitable ravages of time. I judged the results of his accident to be in his legs, which were concealed by a rug drawn closely across his waist. The man's hair was completely white, his complexion parchmentlike, pallid, entirely colorless. His features were so finely cut and chiseled that they resembled a piece of statuary. As the butler announced us and then disappeared and we walked slowly toward him, Hananish smiled in a welcoming fashion that was marred by the bloodless quality of his lips. There was in the twist of his mouth a touch of the spider to the fly quality that destroyed the classic perfection of his features, revealing a tinge of the sadist. I could well imagine him as a back-country despot.

Beautifully shaped hands maneuvered his wheelchair closer to a desk of fruitwood and he indicated adjacent chairs with delicate fingers.

"Do be seated, Mr. Holmes . . . Dr. Watson. I am honored by your presence." As we mumbled suitable greetings, a gentle bewilderment segued into his tone.

"Knowing of the busy and active life you gentlemen lead, I'm at a loss as to how I can assist you. However, there must be something I can do which will become most apparent after Mr. Holmes explains it." His masklike elderly face, singularly devoid of wrinkles, favored me with another tight smile. "I rather lean on your words, Dr. Watson, for you frequently write that all is clear after one of your friend's explanations."

There was a suggestion of Oriental exaggeration in Hananish's loquaciousness, which Holmes chose to cut through.

"I must disappoint you," he said. "Regarding the policy issued by Inter-Ocean on the missing gold shipment, there are some quite ordinary formalities. You know I am investigating the matter for the insurance group."

Hananish nodded. "We are—and I speak for the other financial institutions involved as well as myself—grateful for the policy with Inter-Ocean."

"In what way?"

One white eyebrow, so perfect it might have been plucked, rose questioningly and Holmes continued.

"The gold was turned over to the Birmingham and Northern by your people and was their responsibility until it was delivered to the French."

"Until it was delivered to the French vessel in Great Yarmouth harbor," responded the financier.

There was the suggestion of a "tut-tut" in his voice, which Holmes chose to ignore.

"My point being that if the stolen gold shipment had not been covered by insurance, the railroad would have been responsible."

"It still is. I'm being overly technical, of course. Our banks are to be reimbursed for the worth of the gold by the Birmingham and Northern. If the gold is not found, they will secure the face value of their insurance policy and transfer the money to us. In effect, the money might just as well come to us from Inter-Ocean."

Holmes had been nodding through this rather detailed explanation and I sensed impatience in his manner.

"I am interested in the mechanics of this financial transaction. 'If you would learn, consult the expert' is a worthwhile philosophy," my friend added.

Hananish acknowledged this diplomatic quote with another tight smile that did not reach his eyes. He's a self-styled Caesar, I thought, and it will become common knowledge how he instructed the famous Sherlock Holmes on finance. At least that was how I read the situation then. I learned later I was wrong, no new experience.

"You know of the gold bonds of the Credit Lyonnais?" asked Hananish.

Holmes's expression had a yes and no quality, and the banker explained with a gusto surprising from one so frail.

"To facilitate their rapid sale, the French incorporated a proviso that the bonds could be redeemed two years after their issuance in gold. That's pure mumbo-jumbo. Having the bonds redeemable prior to expiration date might just as well have specified francs, but gold is the lure to the investor. Whenever a currency is troubled people run to gold, which is the ultimate currency."

The man's face had strayed my way and he must have noted a puzzlement for he chose to elaborate on his last sentence.

"You have in your wallet, Doctor, a pound note. Of itself it is valueless, being naught but engraved paper. The fact that it is a medium of exchange for so much gold is what gives it value. The pound sterling is the most stable currency in the world, so it is of no difference whether you have your pound note or its equivalent in gold."

"The note being more convenient to carry," I replied, just to indicate that I was aware of the point he was making.

"Of course. But to the investor, the knowledge that he can cash in his bonds for gold produces a comforting feeling. Gold can be buried and hoarded. It is the constant in the fluctuating world of finance."

"And the French need the metal," stated Holmes.

"The need is artificial," replied Hananish. His manner became that of a patient instructor with two backward students, which, no doubt, delighted him. It crossed my mind that it must have pleased Holmes as well since this information seemed most germane to our case at hand.

"The Credit Lyonnais is a very stable banking house. Because of that cursed Netherlands-Sumatra matter, there was a minor swell of panic in the public mind, which has not as yet subsided. The two-year redemption date is close upon us and the French anticipate that nervous investors will be at their door before long to cash in their bonds prior to the expiration date, as is their right. If investors request payment in gold, the Credit Lyonnais had better have it or suffer a mortal blow to its reputation. Gold, in bulk, flows from country to country dependant on history mostly. During the French Revolution, a lot of the metal found its way here. During the farflung conquests of the Corsican, a lot of it came to France in the same manner as many of their treasures in the Louvre. At one time we were buying heavily from them before the African mines began producing so well. At the moment, English banks have a heavy backlog. When the Credit Lyonnais need became known to me and others, we were glad to enter into an agreement with the French to supply them."

The banker's tapered fingers gestured expressively as though he had made the whole matter as clear as he could.

"A shrewd piece of business, I would hazard," said Holmes. "You could hardly lose unless . . ."

As Holmes's words hung in midair, there was an alarmed reaction from the financier.

"We could *not* lose, Mr. Holmes."

"Then the Birmingham and Northern is capable of reimbursing you for the value of the shipment?"

To my amazement, Hananish actually gaffawed, something I never expected this frigid man to do.

"Mr. Holmes, you jest. Alvidon Chasseur is on the verge of becoming the leading railroad magnate in England. His rise from ownership of a minor trunk line to his present position is a story-book saga akin to the writings of that colonial Horatio Alger. In any case, he had the shipment insured. You know that."

Holmes shrugged. "What about Inter-Ocean? Can they meet the face value of the insurance policy?"

Hananish's unexpected humor disappeared to be replaced by a glacial hauteur. "You make mock of me, Mr. Holmes. You have had dealings with the company. Your solution of the attempted embezzlement by one of their directors is common knowledge. You can hardly think that Inter-Ocean is shaky."

The banker was right, of course, but Holmes wasn't going to let him know it.

"Sir, what I, as a layman, think about such matters may be a far cry from what you, an expert, know."

Hananish had to retreat in the face of this statement. "Of course. Of course. Do forgive me."

Holmes did not abandon the stern look he had adopted, and as the financier rushed ahead, apologetically, I thought, He's done it again. This esthetic dictator would not willingly give the time of day and now he's singing merrily simply because Holmes knew how to wind up his gramophone.

"Perhaps I'd better go over the entire matter," Hananish suggested, and Holmes indicated that this would be acceptable.

"Chasseur's railroad and the Inter-Ocean insurance company are but middlemen in the deal. A consortium of banks, of which I am a member, was well able to make the gold available. The French issued certificates of indebtedness to us for half a million pounds plus a fee." Hananish caught himself and corrected his last statement. "For the equivalent in French francs actually, but that is unimportant. The certificates are convertible, quite as good as currency. With one I could go to any major bank in the world and secure the face value."

"But since the French did not receive the gold, those certificates are not convertible?"

"We shall be reimbursed by the insurance payment."

"Unless the gold is found," I stated, glad to make a comment.

"It is to be hoped that it is," agreed Hananish

quickly. "Otherwise Inter-Ocean is the loser and the thieves the winners."

"If the gold is not found, what will the Credit Lyonnais do?" inquired the sleuth.

"Make an arrangement with someone else. Possibly the Deutsch bank." Again Hananish paused and corrected himself. "Though I am not informed as to their gold reserve at this time. However, the need will be filled." His eyes, a soft shade of blue, swiveled to me briefly and then returned to my friend. "If the subject interests you, might I point out an unusual factor?"

"By all means," replied Holmes.

"Under normal circumstances the gold need not have left our vaults. Upon receipt of the certificates from the Credit Lyonnais, we would have issued demand notes making the gold available to whomsoever presented them. Said notes would go to a French bank, or any European bank for that matter, and would be honored. But psychology enters the scene. The panicky subscriber to the Credit Lyonnais bond issue presents himself at its doors and wants the gold in his hands. He really doesn't need it, you see, but that is the way of the world. Do you follow me?"

Holmes nodded. I did not, but that made no difference.

"This gives me a clear picture of the transaction," stated Holmes. "Dr. Watson and I are grateful, and our trip has proven worthwhile."

As he rose and made as though to depart, Holmes posed another question, a device that I had seen him use on other occasions.

"What happens now to the certificates from the Credit Lyonnais?"

Hananish's thin lips pursed in a moue. "They are

quite worthless, of course, unless you can locate the gold, Mr. Holmes."

"Yes, there still is that possibility," replied my friend. He did not sound enthusiastic, but I discounted this since Holmes was always a superb actor.

At this point we made our departure from the overly quiet, somewhat ominous home of Burton Hananish, who had been maneuvered into giving us a lesson in the mechanics of international finance. Or perhaps he just thought he had.

Chapter 10

❧

The Battle
on the River Road

AGAIN THE pattern of our investigation took a swerve from the norm. Instead of returning to Fenley proper and boarding the first train for London, my friend chose to prolong our west country interlude. He directed our vehicle to the inn and reserved rooms. Something, which had evaded me completely, had gotten the wind up for Holmes since he was never quite comfortable when removed from his beloved London and its teeming millions. Happily, he did not bury himself in thoughtful silence but was disposed to explain his latest move.

"Burton Hananish can bear a long second look, Watson, and while here in Gloucester I will seek answers to questions which come to mind."

"His story seemed straight enough."

"In part, in part."

"The arrangement with the Credit Lyonnais involved a lot of backing and filling. Perhaps it only seemed complex to my untutored mind."

"No, Watson, your point is well taken. If man ever invents the perpetual motion machine, it will have very few working parts. The more spokes and wheels, the greater the possibility of error."

"Or chicanery?" I suggested, keen to learn what had clued Holmes. Surprisingly, his next statement provided an answer.

"Any arrangement where one party cannot lose arouses my suspicions." My friend's voice had a dreamy quality and I knew he was actually talking to himself, using me as the familiar baffle board for his suppositions, which might cement themselves into fact.

"Banks and financial houses are, in essence, service organizations providing capital for expansion, development and presentation of products, creation of new jobs; all of which adds to prosperity. I oversimplify, but that's the nuts and bolts of it. Where currency is involved, loss by whatever means is a universal peril shared by all parties."

"But how could the west coast banks lose in the arrangement that Hananish outlined?" I asked.

"If I judge correctly, the French paid well for the gold they needed. If it were all so foolproof, they would not have had to. Besides, as you observed, the whole matter did seem unwieldy and we'd best unravel it to our satisfaction."

We were by now back at the Red Grouse Inn. Holmes suggested that I might profitably rest my bones and I knew what that meant. He was going to sally forth to investigate on his own, probably with the mysterious though affable Wally. As we washed up in our comfortable suite, I made mention of the man, seeking to draw my friend out. Holmes had one of his fluent evasions ready at hand.

"When dealing with a known ability, names or titles are of scant importance. Now I must check up on several matters which need not involve you, good fellow. The information, like grain in the fields, is but waiting for the gleaner."

Leaning against the doorjamb of Holmes's bed-chamber, I smiled. The picture of my friend searching a harvested field for stray grain struck me as ludicrous until I realized that a detective does often face a similar situation—the poring over of incidents created by some and recounted by others, with an eye always cocked for an overlooked kernel of truth.

Shortly thereafter, Holmes was off and I did get a comfortable nap. I then took myself to the tap room since my friend was not about. With evening coming on, there were more customers present. I posed a few questions about the local fishing conditions during the season. Through my long association with the world's greatest detective, I had learned that this was a safe approach. Speak to one who knows anything about fish and you automatically become the audience for his tale of the one that got away. Whilst the story has a boring sameness, it shields the listener from questions regarding his presence and the reason for it. I exchanged words with some of the locals, lost a few coins at the dart board as befits a newcomer to an area, and passed my time pleasantly but without profit. The opportunity to guide the conversation around to Burton Hananish did not present itself.

When Holmes did return and locate me, I was quite ready to join him for dinner. It was at this point that my original estimate of the management of the Red Grouse was upheld, for Holmes and I dined not well but sumptuously.

Holmes chose a bottle of fine old brown brandy, very reasonable at five and two, to top off our feast. As a result, I slept very soundly that night despite my late afternoon nap.

The following morning, when I finally forced my eyes apart, things were rather inconvenient since we had not planned to spend the night in Fenley. But I brushed off my traveling suit and found a serviceable straightedge, no doubt on loan from the landlord. Holmes was not about. It occurred to me that my friend had found much of interest in Fenley, for he had obviously been up and about at an early hour.

I decided to take a brief stroll. When I reached the street, a closed carriage was pulling up at the inn. I paused to allow the door to open and was jostled from behind. When I turned instinctively, the carriage door did open and, of a sudden, there was a large palm across my mouth, stifling the cry that rose in my throat. The man who had come up behind me had my wrists pinioned in a steely grasp and I found myself rudely deposited on the floor of the carriage. An adhesive strip was affixed over my mouth, my arms were secured with rough twine that had the smell of hemp about it, a blindfold was over my eyes, and the carriage was under way. Completely surprised and appalled though I was, I had to admire the efficiency with which my captors had pulled it off. My reluctant approval lessened when the driver, at a signal or by plan, whipped up the horse and we were outward bound from Fenley at a rapid rate. This made little sense since I had been taken with no fuss at all and they would have been better advised to proceed quietly on their way so as to arouse no comment or suspicion. There were mutterings between what I assumed were two men, and my hat was taken from my head. There was the sound of a window of the conveyance being lowered.

"That does it," stated one voice. "It's plain as day in the road."

They must have cast my hat from the carriage, which was ridiculous, for my initials, J.H.W., were plainly stamped on the sweat band. Perhaps I was being victimized by a crew of amateurs, but I could not accept that thought.

It was highly uncomfortable bouncing on the floorboards of the carriage and possibly our trip seemed longer than it actually was.

Finally, we pulled to a stop and I was removed from the vehicle with little ceremony. As they marched me with insistent prodding, the thongs on my wrists were cut and I received a violent shove from behind, which propelled me down two stone steps. I lost my footing and fell resoundingly on a cold stone floor, bruising one kneecap painfully in the process. As I lay there for a moment, stifling an exclamation of pain and feeling the fool indeed for being such an easy prey, there was the clang of a door behind me and I was alone—far from the comforting presence of Holmes, in completely strange surroundings, and captured for reasons unknown. There was a stab of fear in my heart that was promptly washed away by anger. Grabbed off, I was like a helpless child and without even an idea of the doers, for if the sleuth had appeared at that very moment I could have given him no clear description of the men involved, the direction we had taken, or the distance traversed. It had to dawn on me that this was a ridiculous situation for a middle-aged general practitioner to find himself in and undeniable proof that I was ill-fitted to dog the footsteps of the world's greatest detective and brave the dangers inevitable because of his profession. However, the practicality of my Scottish mother came to the fore. The riches of the Indies could not move the second hand of time backward and my situation had to be accepted or else I must seek refuge in the unreal world of the mentally unstable, a retreat that offered no satisfaction, though I did feel somewhat daft for allowing all this to happen.

With a groan, I stumbled to my feet, tearing the blindfold from my eyes. That was easy enough, but the adhesive gag was another matter. I pulled it swiftly, losing some skin and a bit of my moustache as well.

The walls of my dungeon were of stone, like the floor. A quick inspection revealed no crumbling masonry, and they appeared stout enough to withstand the onslaught of tools had I any available. Light came from a window set high in the thick walls and it was, alas, heavily barred, though I was in doubt if I could have gotten through the opening anyway. The room was damp and there was the smell of the river nearby. The only piece of furniture was a simple bed of modern design, metal in fact, on which one grubby blanket was thrown. It took but a moment to move the bed under the window at the far wall. Stepping up on the framework of the bed, I was able to look outside. The outer wall of my prison was right on the Severn, and by craning my neck and standing on tip toes, I could see water washing against its base. The bars were of iron, firmly set in concrete. From the position of the building, I felt that it was part of the ruins of an ancient fort built at the headwaters of the Severn to repel the Norsemen, and reconstructed through the centuries for a variety of reasons. Judging from the lack of sound other than the washing of the river and occasional bird calls, it had to be in an uninhabited area. My survey of the outside world complete and frustrating, I devoted my attention to the door at my prison chamber. It was formed of stout timbers secured by iron headed bolts. The hinges were massive and designed to defy an escape attempt. Set in the frame on each side of the door were two L-shaped metal forms that puzzled me momentarily. Then I realized that the structure had originally been designed to keep intruders out rather than secure prisoners within. There was no cross bar available to place in them to secure the door, but while it might have frustrated my captors, it would have done me no good. What I wanted to do was escape, not remain. I tried to open the door with little hope, and of course I was right since it withstood my violent tugging. Breathing deeply and gnawing at my moustache with nervous teeth, I tried to analyze the situation as Holmes would have.

Unlike most of the sleuth's part and full-time employees, I had no hidden weapon on my person. I was outnumbered, with little chance of overpowering my captors. The silence indicated that they had locked me up and left, possibly on some other nefarious mission. Were this so, they would not have secreted me in a spot where a cry for help would be heard or heeded. I could try a call or two but that might bring back the ruffians, something I did not relish at the moment. The great sleuth on one occasion had mentioned that man was forced to make do with what he had. Besides my clothes, I had my wallet, which had not been taken from me. I had a pocket handkerchief, clean, and the monocle I carried but seldom used, though it was of occasional assistance in deciphering small print. There were coins and keys in my pockets along with a half-consumed packet of cigarettes and matches. I might attempt to ignite the blanket on the bed, but I doubted if I could get the material to burn and the result, if successful, might just be my own suffocation. In despair, I got atop the bed again to peer through the window. The Severn was broad at this point and there was occasional river traffic. While the water looked deep right up to the river's edge, what vessels were in sight were a good distance offshore and far beyond the range of my voice. It occurred to me that even if I could reach by sound a passing boat, they would be unable to locate me on the shoreline. There was my handkerchief. Might I not tie it to one of the bars as a guide to some observant soul alerted by my cries? I was considering this possibility with a little enthusiasm when there was the sound of the door quietly opening behind me.

I whirled around, ready to face my captors and if possible leave my mark upon them, but to my complete astonishment it was a familiar who glided silently through the door and eased it shut behind him.

I was gazing into the fathomless green eyes of Wakefield Orloff.

Suddenly my despair vanished like a canary from a magician's hat. True, it was not the invincible Holmes who had come to my rescue, but in my friend's absence, it was he who, above all others, I would choose to extract me from a sticky situation. I felt light-headed, giddy at the thought of what would happen if my captors returned and the deadly security agent with his steel-rimmed hat and arsenal of weapons went to work. Were there ten of the ruffians, Orloff would sweep them aside, and in a lethal manner to boot, for I had seen him in action and there were none that could stand against him. As these thoughts flooded my brain, my mouth must have dropped open but I smothered an utterance at a gesture of warning from that completely frightening man who was, thank God, my friend.

He was at my side in a moment, gazing anxiously into my eyes, which might have been a bit moist in honor of our opportune reunion.

"Are you all right, Doctor? Holmes will never forgive me if harm has come to you."

"Aside from a bruised knee, minor contusions, and a damaged ego, tip-top, old chap." My voice echoed bravado for I was no longer the paunchy doctor but, in my mind's eye, a veritable D'Artagnan. Bravery comes easily when one walks with an armored column.

"Then we'd best be gone. I'll deal with those who took you later." Even I, his ally, felt a chill at the grim finality in the agent's voice, but a greater chill followed this as we both heard a key turn in the lock. Orloff flew to the door, but it withstood even his strength. There was the sound of a chuckle from beyond the portal and then a mocking voice.

"Rest easy, Mr. Holmes. We'll attend to you and your companion later."

Then there was silence as my eyes met with Orloff's. He returned, with a shrug, from the door. My heart sank but then curiosity reared its insistent head.

"What does this all mean?" I queried in a hushed voice.

"They baited a trap and sprung it at the wrong time." Orloff amended this. "Actually they had no choice. Even if they knew I was not Holmes, which they did not, they couldn't have me nosing around."

I shook my head in complete confusion and chided myself for being so obtuse.

"I'm left at the starting gate, dear chap."

As he explained, Orloff's eyes were surveying our cell, and he moved around it on an inspection tour much like the one I had undertaken.

"They grabbed you outside the inn but made sure
that your hat remained as evidence. The moment I
realized you were missing, it took little time to find
the hat and to learn of a closed carriage that left
Fenley by the river road with a whirl of wheels and
a cloud of dust. Picking up the trail was no great
thing, but when I located this place it seemed
deserted, which was their intention."

I had begun to nod at his re-creation. "I was the
bait, then, to lure Holmes to this spot and bag us
both."

"They did not anticipate my presence and even
now think their ruse has succeeded."

"What are you doing here, by the way?"

Atop the bed, looking toward the river, Orloff
shot me a glance over his shoulder. "Mr. Holmes
always takes care of his own."

His response might have seemed enigmatic but I
understood. Tiny and Burlington Bertie, even now,
were guarding 221 B Baker Street, and when
Holmes left me to my own devices in Fenley, it was
with the reassurance that the world's most dangerous man was watching out for my interests.

I discovered a catch in my throat as I thought of
my eccentric, bohemian friend who could be a trial
to live with but who was always concerned about
the well-being of the plodding, phlegmatic companion cast his way by fate and the presence of
young Stamford at the Criterion Bar on that certain day that had become so significant to J. H.
Watson and Sherlock Holmes.

As I recovered from my momentary emotion,
Orloff's death-dealing hands had seized the bars of
the windows and the back of his coat tightened as
those amazing shoulders, biceps, and wrists were
put to work. At first glance, or even second, Orloff
was completely misleading in appearance. He was

unusually broad, though one did not realize it because of his grace of movement. His width made him seem shorter than he was, while his round, almost moon-shaped face gave the impression of a somewhat overweight man. There was not an ounce of surplus flesh on him, for his bulk was solid muscle augmented by reflexes that defied my medically trained mind. He was Orloff, cast from some unknown mold that no master hand could recreate. Suddenly his swelling muscles relaxed and he turned from the bars without a trace of moisture of his brow and breathing in his regular, even cadence.

As his eyes flashed around our place of confinement, I realized that he had given up on the window and was looking elsewhere for a way out. Concentrating on the single furnishing of this barren place, the security agent elevated the bed from the floor and was gazing at its underpinnings. There might have been a trace of satisfaction in his expression as he cast the blanket and thin pallet in a corner and studied the two angle bars and two smaller cross pieces that formed the rectangular frame.

"You have a thought?" I asked.

The man nodded, gesturing toward the door. "They don't want us out, and for the moment, we don't want them in."

He had the frame separated in a moment and, taking one of the angle bars, he crossed to the door and placed it laterally in the two attachments I had noted previously.

"Not as wide as the original timber bar but 'twill do," he said with satisfaction, crossing back to the window. "We'll need something to signal with, for our rescue will come from the river."

How he knew this I could not guess, but I

displayed my pocket handkerchief. "Will this do?" From his expression I deduced that it would not. "It is all I have save my monocle."

Orloff's green eyes brightened. Seizing the eyepiece, he cast a rapid glance at the sunlight coming through the cell window.

"Should work," he stated in a matter-of-fact way. He surveyed my figure with a speculative manner. "Could you balance me on your shoulders, Doctor, for I've got to be at the window level."

Doubt was dominant in my mind, and expression as well, for muscle weighs more than fat and I judged that Orloff tipped the scales at fifteen stone. Sensing my thought, he nodded.

"There's another way." Suddenly he sprang for the window, one hand grasping a bar. Orloff never jumped, for in motion, he always resembled a ballet star. With part of his weight supported by one hand, I sensed what he had in mind and got his legs around my shoulders, standing beneath him to provide some support. Even with Orloff taking most of his weight on his arm of steel, my leg muscles began to tremble after a while and I was forced to let my rescuer down several times so that I could recover. I knew what he was doing, of course. Using the lens of my monocle to reflect sunlight, he was sending intermittent signals toward passing boats in hopes of attracting someone's eye. Finally, our efforts were rewarded.

"We've been spotted," he said. "A boat is swerving in toward shore."

"Thank heavens for that," I said, my shirt soaked with perspiration and my breath coming in gasps.

Orloff signaled for me to allow him to drop to the floor.

"Providence has been doubly generous since it is Holmes," he stated, returning my monocle. Again he sprang upward but this time he had two hands free and was able to hold himself at window height with ease.

While I wondered what had alerted the sleuth to use the river, Orloff kept me informed as to happenings.

"Evidently he commandeered a river tug and she's fast closing on us." The throb of powerful engines was an accompaniment to his words but they suddenly diminished and I sensed the river boat was near to shore.

"Holmes, it is Orloff," called the security agent.

"What of Watson?" Though from a distance, I thought I sensed a tremor in my friend's voice.

"With me and all right."

"Anyone else around?"

"Don't know. If they are hidden out front, this noise must have alerted them. I'd keep an eye cocked."

After a short pause, Holmes spoke again. "I'll work my way around to the road and try and release you."

"Wait," I cried. "There could be too many of them."

"I've another thought," called the security agent to Holmes, "if you've a stout line available and the means of getting it to us."

There was a mumble of voices from the river and then Holmes replied.

"That can be done. You've a mind to try the window."

Orloff did not answer but motioned for me to stand clear of the aperture, though I was well below it. Perhaps my nerves were playing me tricks, but I thought I sensed movement from beyond the door to our place of confinement. Suddenly Orloff pulled himself as close to the window as possible and his right hand snaked between the bars, reaching outward. In a moment it reappeared with a round object clutched in his fingers. I recognized it as the weighted end of a heaving line as Orloff dropped to the floor, reeling in the light line. Motioning toward the other angle bar of the demolished bed frame, Orloff pulled in the end of a hawser to which the heaving line had been attached with a running hitch. He took the piece of the bed frame from me, running the hawser around it. The sound of the tug's engines had picked up tempo and I sensed that she was being maneuvered around to present her stern to the shoreline. Orloff had the hawser secured around the angle bar with an anchor bend and he pulled himself up to the window, placing the bar across the width of the opening. There was the sound of a key turning a lock and the door behind us opened slightly but the cross bar held it firmly and there was a muffled curse and then a crash as a body tried to force it inward.

"Full speed," shouted Orloff. There was a deep-throated roar from the tug's engines and the hawser tightened, pulling the frame piece of the bed against the window bars. Outside, the boat's engines were protesting with wheezes and clankings, trying with twin screws to force the tug into motion. Orloff, hanging from the window by one hand, reached down and grasped me under the arm with his other. Suddenly I was in the air.

"Grab 'round my neck, Doctor, and hold on for dear life."

How he got me up to where I could obey his order I'll never know. There were repeated crashes at the door to our rear and suddenly there was a rending sound and a section of the wall including the window and bars gave way to the power of the tug's engines. We were in the open air with stone and the dry dust of masonry around us and plunging toward the water below. All I could do was cling to Orloff, who in turn kept his grip on the bars, which were attached to the hawser. We hit the water but were not allowed to sink, for the tug, released from the anchor that had held it, was racing from the shoreline at high speed and dragging us behind it. Suddenly the ship's engines were cut and a stubby man with a mahogany face appeared at the stern of the craft and began hauling us toward it. There was the crash of an explosion and then another one and I made haste to swim toward the tug, sensing that the ruffians had broken down the cell door and were firing on us. When Orloff and the short man helped me aboard, I saw Holmes standing by the wheelhouse with a long-barreled revolver, firing methodically toward the shore. Coughing up river water, I cast a glance toward our rear. Fully a third of the wall of an aged blockhouse was torn asunder. As I watched, a face appeared in the aperture and ducked promptly as Holmes's revolver barked and there was a spurt of dust and the whine of a ricocheting bullet.

He's got them pinned down, I thought. Orloff and I have escaped, and Holmes is alive and well. Merry old England will survive.

Chapter 11

❧

Back to Baker Street

It was several hours later that I lay luxuriating in a steaming hot bath. Holmes had secured fresh shirts and undergarments from the local haberdasher, and the innkeeper's wife was ironing my sodden suit. The river tug had deposited us at the Fenley docks, and when Holmes had pressed a considerable payment on the captain, he met with some resistance. That worthy confessed that he had not enjoyed himself so much since he helped run down two escaped prisoners from the Coleford jail who were making for Cardiff in a stolen launch. Holmes had been insistent and had given the lively old sailor a personal card with a number penned on the back.

"Should there be questions from the local authorities," my friend had said, "have them contact this number at Whitehall."

"Pshaw," the mahogany-faced captain had responded. "I'll just show 'em your card and that will shut 'em up." Such are the benefits of fame.

By the time I had toweled off, Orloff joined us in our suite at the Red Grouse Inn. He appeared as calm and polished as though he had spent the morning lecturing the local ladies' sewing circle on the care of ailing cats. Holmes had me swathed in a blanket with a tot of Irish whiskey in my hand, and his solicitude drew a small smile from the security agent and a tinge of warmth entered his normally cold, unemotional green eyes. With Orloff on hand, Holmes bustled off to secure my suit, which allowed me to pose a question or two. Mycroft Holmes's right-hand man and his most feared agent always treated Sherlock Holmes with deference, for he was so good himself that he could recognize greatness in others. With me he exhibited flashes of humor and actual friendship, something I would reveal to no one, for I would be courting disbelief. The shadowy enforcer of the espionage system that officially did not exist was reputed to have all the friendly tendencies of a prowling Bengal tiger. Why he should present a different face toward me was a mystery I was incapable of solving.

"I say," I mouthed as a curtain raiser, "you never did tell me how you chanced to be down this way."

"The matter of gold and the solidarity of the pound is of interest to Her Majesty's government," he replied, igniting one of the small black cigars he fancied. He was just talking and knew that I saw through his answer that answered nothing. Holmes had asked his brother for Orloff, and Mycroft Holmes had complied as he had done in the past. Now I could identify the associate of Holmes that the mysterious Wally had referred to in the tap-room the previous afternoon. Which brought me to the matter I really wanted to touch upon.

"You're down here smoothing the way for that Wally chap."

"You've met him, then?" Orloff seemed mildly surprised.

"Very briefly. Don't even know his name or occupation either, but Holmes seems to place great store by him. I'd say he's giving the fellow a free rein, for he provided no instructions during our short meeting."

"On the theory that some knowledge can be inconvenient, Holmes hasn't chosen to tell you about the gentleman. All right, Doctor, I'll spin you a tale that will be our secret, though it's just a story dealing with no particular person we know."

I must have leaned forward with a pleased expression, for Holmes did tend to have his little mysteries and nothing delighted me more than to be one up on him.

"You've heard, perhaps, of the confidence game?" asked Orloff, blowing smoke toward the ceiling.

"Bunko, they call it," I replied. "Bogus companies, non-existent stock, manipulators who prey on the larceny that lurks in most hearts."

Again Orloff registered surprise. "That's an apt remark, for a flim-flam man wouldn't get a farthing from a truly honest citizen. But no matter. Who, would you say, is the king of the con men?"

"Get Rich Quick Wallingford," I responded promptly. "The exploits of the American are known far and . . ." My voice dwindled away and I stared at Orloff, noting the slight smile teasing the corners of his mouth. "Wally," I muttered softly, "I see."

"The man *you* referred to, not I, has no warrants outstanding in the States, though I'm sure the American police would be delighted if he no longer graced their shores. Now, England is a small nation, though many of our people have served, in times gone by, under foreign flags as mercenaries."

"We've hired a few ourselves on occasion," I

stated, my mind reverting to the revolution of the Colonies and the battle of Trenton.

"Exactly. Now if such a man as you mentioned were to come over here because the climate in his homeland was too warm, possibly his wide experience could be put to use for the benefit of society."

"To catch a thief . . ." I muttered, and then my mouth snapped shut. I did not wish to pursue the subject for fear that one of us might say too much. Rather, I resorted to the matter at hand.

"But who is the thief?"

"There has to be one for there's a half a million that's missing."

It was at this moment that Holmes rejoined us, and by the time I had donned my now presentable outer garments, Wally appeared as well. So it's to be a war council, I thought, regarding the American's handsome face with added respect.

Holmes put the ball in play without a warm-up. "We've hit on to something," he stated, filling his short briar, "for Watson was captured today and they were after me as well."

Wally's face registered momentary consternation. "Could it be because of what I'm doing? Surely not, for our brief meeting yesterday could have caused no suspicion."

A sudden thought flashed through my mind. Could the Red Grouse Inn be part of the widespread apparatus controlled by Mycroft Holmes, the second most powerful man in England? I abandoned the idea.

Sherlock Holmes, his pipe lit, agreed with Wally. "No, I think your activites have been well covered." His eyes shifted toward Orloff. "No chance of a leak, is there?"

Orloff responded in the negative. "The bank

examiner we are using doesn't really know what's
going on. As for the teller, I have too much on him."

So, I thought, some old debts are being paid off.

Holmes seated himself in the armchair. "I think
the sudden attention that came our way was the
result of our meeting with Burton Hananish."

"Which confirms your suspicions regarding
him," said Wally.

"Oh, he has to be a part of it, though possibly
unwittingly." My friend seemed very certain on this
point. "What I'd like to know is what alerted
Hananish or someone in his household to the
presence of danger and brought about the attack on
Watson."

"You discussed the mechanics of the gold shipment, of course." The American Wally's warm,
gregarious manner was diminished by a glitter in
his clear and forthright eyes.

Holmes nodded. "Hananish went over the reason
the French needed the gold, the certificates of
indebtedness issued by them to the west coast
banks . . ."

My friend would have continued, but something
in Wally's manner caused him to fall silent. There
was a weighty pause. Wally was leaning forward in
his chair regarding Holmes like an Irish setter
ready to put up a bird.

"Certificate of indebtedness, you say, Mr.
Holmes? Now what might that be?"

Holmes seemed momentarily nonplussed. "Like
a letter of credit, perhaps?"

"I can understand the meaning though I'm not
familiar with the term, but the French have no
need for such paper. Like the Bank of England, the
Credit Lyonnais has the power to issue currency
that is just as convertible as this country's Bank of
England notes."

Wally's statement prompted a groan from Orloff. "I do hope this matter does not involve the Prescott plates, for the C.I.D. is still experiencing nightmares regarding them."

By this time I was scratching my head in a bewildered fashion, and as he did so often, Holmes noticed my puzzlement.

"A counterfeiter named Prescott is said to have created plates capable of producing Bank of England notes that would defy inspection anywhere. Prescott was shot to death by an American criminal, and his engravings have never been located."* Holmes turned back to Wally.

"You feel the certificates Hananish mentioned are so much rigamarole?"

"Not necessarily, but it doesn't sound right. Let us pose a model situation in a framework of one on one. You," he pointed to Holmes, "are the Hananish bank while I am the Credit Lyonnais. You have the gold and prepare for its actual delivery, an unusual situation."

"Hananish pointed that out," said Holmes.

"I arrange payment with legal tender, undoubtedly using Credit Lyonnais bank notes. These certificates of indebtedness imply a mortgage, chattel, which is not the case. You're selling, I'm buying."

Had Holmes's aquiline nose been capable, it certainly would have been quivering at this point. Yet he indulged in a lengthy silence, finally breaking it with a suggestion.

"Let us proceed with Hananish's explanation of the matter."

---

*Obviously this adventure predates the matter of the Three Garridebs, in which Holmes not only captured Killer Evans, the man who shot the counterfeiter, but also recovered the Prescott plates.

"It may be dead on," admitted the American. "Financial houses can become mired down with unnecessary complexities while inefficient ones dote on them."

"The gold is gathered by the consortium of banks. Trelawney is involved, possibly Michaels, and certainly Hananish." Holmes shot a glance at Orloff and I suspected that there had been discussion about the possible connection among the three men named. "The gold is ready for shipment and the bankers are in receipt of the legal tender; certificates, or whatever, from the Credit Lyonnais."

"How did that happen?" asked Wally bluntly.

"Hananish said it did."

"According to him, the French have paid for something they do not have." For the first time, Wally's homeland became apparent in his style of speech. "I mean, we're all friends together and all that. Everybody trusts everybody else, but doesn't it seem a mite casual?"

"When viewed in that light, it does," admitted the sleuth.

"Something's amiss in Denmark, Mr. Holmes," said Wally, misquoting.

"Rotten," I said.

"What?" queried the American.

"I was just . . . never mind." I wished I'd kept silent.

Though we had arrived at a breakthrough and something specific for the confidence expert to explore, Holmes was not prepared to abandon the matter.

"How would you arrange this matter?" he asked Wally. "On the up and up, of course." Evidently, Holmes regretted his last sentence for he shot me a quick glance. Fortunately, I was able to preserve a bland expression.

Wally had a ready answer. "The gold is ready for shipment. On behalf of the Credit Lyonnais, I would make payment to the west coast banks when the Inter-Ocean insurance policy is made out in favor of the Credit Lyonnais. That way if the gold is not delivered, the French banking firm is covered for the entire period of the transaction."

"Hananish said the insurance policy was made out to the Birmingham and Northern, which was committed to turn it over to the west coast banks if the gold disappeared."

"Did he, now? Then Hananish and his banking cronies had the French payment and the gold and in addition were covered by the Inter-Ocean insurance policy."

In spite of myself, I found words again. "Hananish stated specifically that the French certificates became valueless if the gold shipment was stolen."

The American exhibited a wise smile that had the good grace not to seem condescending. "I'm willing to accept the possibility that the French issued some sort of dated certificates that cease to be convertible if the gold shipment does not cross the Channel. It's cumbersome, but not all things are done the easy way. Even so, for a brief period, the bankers here have half a million in gold and also something more than that in Credit Lyonnais notes. A million pounds all told and when you are dealing with that much money, a day or even an hour can make a big difference."

Faced with such logic, I could do naught but agree. "And they were insured as well, as you pointed out," I said.

"We certainly have meat for the table of thought here," said Holmes, and I knew he was fascinated by the possibilites that had opened up. "Our visit to the financier bore richer dividends than we expected, Watson. Perhaps it was worth the difficulties you encountered later."

Noting my gesture of agreement, Holmes's attention returned to the American. "We seem to have explored the matter of Burton Hananish thoroughly. Do you have anything to mention?"

"Yes and it makes more sense now that there is the aroma of stale fish in the air." Wally's eyes shifted to Orloff briefly. "A chance remark by your friend the bank examiner put me on to something just before coming here. Hananish may be trading very heavily in gold, for he just might have sold four hundred thousand pounds' worth to the Deutsch Bank."

Holmes's noble head, lowered in thought, suddenly jerked upward. Orloff looked puzzled.

"What does that have to do with this French situation?"

"Probably nothing, but for a small bank Hananish is certainly active in precious metals. I don't know whether this German sale was made through the consortium of banks or not. If Hananish transacted it solo, he has a lot of gold available."

Holmes's voice was never calmer, but there was a bright light in his eyes.

"When Watson and I spoke with him, the financier mentioned that the Credit Lyonnais might go to the Deutsch Bank for the gold it now needs. He was quick to cover up the statement, but those were his words."

Wally had bounded to his feet, his handsome face aglow.

"Are you thinking what I'm thinking, Mr. Holmes?"

"I imagine we are all savoring the idea," responded the sleuth. "A half a million is stolen from the Birmingham and Northern flyer, and of a sudden, Hananish has four hundred thousand available to sell to the Germans."

"We've got him, Mr. Holmes," exclaimed the American. "He's nailed to the cross."

"But we shall follow the diplomatic adage and make haste slowly," said my friend in a cautionary manner. Of course he was stimulated, nay downright excited. He had to be, for it would seem that detailed investigation, a careful sifting of facts, and a meticulous piecing together of the pieces of a puzzle had paid off again. All the things that Holmes had lectured me on since our first coming together had again proved their worth, but my intimate friend was always intent on tightening the net until not a minnow could escape.

His keen face centered on Orloff. "First we must check the amount of gold that Hananish might have access to." Now the sleuth's eyes speared the ebullient American. "The details of the Deutsch Bank sale can be secured, I'm sure."

Wally, who had recovered his composure, nodded.

"And now, Watson and I must return to London on the evening train for there is a shooting match between the Bagatelle Club rifle squad and Alvidon Chasseur's Wellington Club team."

Both Orloff and Wally looked befuddled at this sudden switch of subjects, and Holmes elaborated with a chuckle.

"From the very beginning of this tangled skein, the army, in an unofficial way, has been in evidence. The late Ezariah Trelawney and Ramsey Michael were veterans of the Crimea War, as is Burton Hananish. The security chief of the B & N railroad was formerly with the army of India.

Lastly, the robbery of the Birmingham and Northern flyer was planned like a military maneuver, while a number of big businesses are hiring former army personnel for their expertise with firearms. I do not choose to accept this as a coincidence. Come, Watson, we'd best make ready for our journey to London." There was a pleased lilt to Holmes's voice, for he was returning to Baker Street.

Chapter 12

&

At the Wellington Gun Club

ON THE train back from Gloucester, Holmes was wrapped up in his thoughts. I did not intrude on them, feeling that he was planning his next move. While he had made mention of the marksmanship contest, surely there were more leads to be followed and Holmes could not have anticipated the results of our journey to the west coast.

We were approaching Reading when the sleuth roused himself from a thoughtful silence and seemed disposed to discuss the matter, which found great favor with me, as I had my usual assortment of questions.

"Watson, there's more to it, you know." He was gazing out the window at the passing countryside, and I forced myself to smother a banal response like, "There is?"

"But we should be thankful for that," he continued.

Confound it, I thought. Where is his mind taking him now?

"The simple matters are the most frustrating."

"How so?"

"Recall, if you will, that Jack the Ripper fellow. Back in 'eighty-eight, it was."

"I'm not likely to forget him. But you can't consider those brutal murders a simple affair."

Holmes turned from our carriage window with surprise in his eyes. "Was there any indication that the Ripper even knew his victims?"

"Well, the killings were most all in Whitechapel."

"But no one was uncovered who had known the seven poor souls and could have been the murderer."

"What is your point?"

"The matter of Jack the Ripper was basically a simple one."

"Oh come now, he was never found. There was much hue and cry that you should be put on the case."

An expression of distaste crossed Holmes's features. "I well remember those newspaper stories— all motivated by a desire for sensationalism, which our press is not averse to. They were certainly not the result of honest conviction unless written by idiots, which is within the realm of possibility."

"Your use of *simple* jars me."

"I did not say easy. The fact is that the street-walker murders were committed with no thought of profit or gain. They were wanton killings by an insane person to fulfill some inner compulsion. What was the prime clue? The occupation of the victims, somehow tied in with the force that drove the Ripper to raw murder. How could I have been of service in the matter? Catching him required a dragnet effort—the searching of doctor's records to locate someone with a deranged mind who might have been impelled to launch a vendetta against prostitutes. The far-flung facilities of Scotland Yard were much more suited for a search of that type than you or I, Watson."

"You feel, then, that he will never be caught?"

"Unless he starts up again—a possibility. Or unless he makes some deathbed confession, which I think is very doubtful."

I shrugged and my mind took an obvious tack.

"How is this associated with the treasure train?"

"Ah, that matter is beset with complexities. But the more angles to a case, the more chance for the lunge of the rapier that will impale the kernel of truth, the key to unlock the door of mystery."

"If complexities aid your investigation, you have plenty."

"Agreed. Had a group of thieves with access to inside information raided the train and removed the gold, we would have had little to work with. How did they get their information? What disposition did they make of the bullion? As it is, I feel this case embraces a wider canvas."

"It certainly does if the Trelawney and Michael deaths are part of the plot."

"That, Watson, will be settled for us. If Cedric Folks killed Michael, then I must abandon my redheaded-man theory."

"Not without regrets," I hazarded. "You do seem quite taken by the idea."

"Because of a remark you made, good fellow."

As I regarded him with puzzlement, he chuckled. "Ah, you haven't figured it out yet. No matter, since for the moment it is a dead issue. Our thoughts must go elsewhere."

"Where, specifically?" I queried, with a show of impatience.

"If Hananish, the banker, is the mastermind, he certainly was not directly involved in the train robbery."

"A man in a wheelchair? I should think not."

"Who, then, did the actual deed? I mean to bag them all, Watson. You recall that when Moriarty went down, the Yard allowed him to escape, along with two of his top henchmen. It was several years later that we convicted Colonel Moran. Then, in that Golden Bird affair, Chu San Fu was not brought to justice and he rose again to plague us. We'll make a clean sweep of it this time, old friend."

That happy prospect caused Holmes to fall silent again, and I could get no more from him during our return trip.

The following morning, we had scarcely completed our morning repast when a despondent Inspector MacDonald was ushered into our quarters. The Scot's habitually glum expression was more pronounced than usual.

"I'll not be guessin' how you figured it, Mr. Holmes, but you did give me fair warning," he said, lowering himself into our cane-backed chair.

"The matter of Cedric Folks," stated Holmes.

"Exactly. I located the artist without much trouble. Of course he denied any association with Michael's death, though he was honest enough to admit that he was not grief-stricken over the happening. But he couldn't come up with an alibi for the time of the murder. Were I a gambling man, I'd have given rather long odds on his being the culprit. Then I ran into a roadblock."

"The hansom driver who had come to the Michael mansion."

MacDonald threw me a dark look. "There's little I can tell him, is there?"

"Come now, Mr. Mac, your case against Folks revolved around the hansom driver. Both Watson and I knew you would track him down straight a-way." As Holmes continued in his soothing tone, I poured the inspector a cup of coffee, which he accepted with gratitude.

"The driver did not identify Folks as his red-headed passenger, I take it."

"For a fact, Mr. Holmes. I was a mite stern with him, bein' somewhat taken aback; but he stood his ground. Said the man in his hansom had a longer nose than Folks; and the color of his hair wasn't the same, bein' more auburn than red."

"The cabbie certainly wasn't color-blind," I remarked.

"I see your point," said Holmes quickly.

This surprised me, for I did not know I'd made one.

"Auburn is an unusual word for a cabbie to use, but no matter. The point is that the case against Cedric Folks has evaporated."

"Completely," agreed MacDonald, lighting up a cigar, which I had secured for him. "Now I'm back where I started."

"Hardly," replied Holmes. "We do know that Michael's ward was not involved, the assassin being the cabbie's passenger. It is possible that I may be able to unearth something about him. Just yesterday I was speaking to Watson about the fall of Moriarty."

I sensed that the sleuth was choosing his words carefully, for MacDonald had been completely hoodwinked by the master criminal's college-professor facade.

"The professor met his end in Switzerland, and we got Moran in connection with that Ronald Adair matter. But one man of the Moriarty ring is still at large."

"Porlock," exclaimed MacDonald.

"No, the informer is free as a convenience. An

arrangement you know of, Mr. Mac. I refer to the late professor's hatchet man."

"Lightfoot," breathed MacDonald. " 'Tis said he died on the Continent."

"No body was found."

As Holmes and the Scot mused on this, I rallied my thoughts. The name meant nothing to me, but I could deduce who they were referring to. Holmes had specifically said that he had spent his years in self-imposed exile from London because two particularly vindictive members of Moriarty's infamous crew had escaped. Sebastian Moran was one, and this Lightfoot fellow must have been the other.

"What makes you suspect McTigue?" asked the inspector.

So, I thought, that's the rascal's name.

Holmes seemed to read my mind. "He used a number of names, and you'll recall that Moriarty only sent him on special assignments. He'd appear at the victim's home as a chimney sweep, a deacon of the church, and on one occasion, he masqueraded as a nurse. A clever felow was Lightfoot, and I've a thought that he's adopted a redheaded disguise and is back in business again. But there is no concrete proof of this."

MacDonald rose with alacrity. "We've a few people who are helpful on occasion that date back to the Moriarty days. I'll be asking some questions about McTigue and checkin' out his supposed death as well."

The inspector departed forthwith. Given a lead, he needed little urging.

I was completely befuddled by this revelation of Holmes's, and he did not seem disposed to discuss it. Something had alerted my friend to the possibility of the presence of an old enemy, but there were so many ifs involved that he had to be playing a hunch. This was contrary to his usual style; and if pressed, I knew he would resort to evasions. Actually, further discussion of the matter was not practical, since Holmes informed me he had an invitation to the rifle contest at the Wellington Club. Not long thereafter we departed for this plaything of the rich and titled.

It was a bit of a trip to the establishment, situated in Bermondsey, close-on to the Deptford Reach curve in the Thames. I realized immediately that the Wellington Gun Club served a variety of purposes, boasting a tip-top grill room, with an adjacent area suitable for the playing of cards. A hideaway where business leaders could consort with their own kind, and I assumed that many a deal had been broached within its stately walls. On this day the club was crowded. It took no brilliance to realize that the match had become an excuse for ladies to don their latest finery and gentlemen, who would not have known a breech from a bolt, to hobnob with the upper strata of society. There was a great to-do about invitations, and there were even some who were denied admission; but the engraved card presented by Holmes secured immediate entry and a carte blanche obsequiousness from the majordomo guarding the entrance. It crossed my mind that we might be present by royal patronage, since Holmes was summoned to Buckingham from time to time, usually after one of his masterly actions on behalf of the Empire. Few indeed were the elite functions that he could not attend if he wished. A humorous *droit civil*, since Holmes was rather antisocial and, contrary to those around us, availed himself of few of the opportunities open to him.

Lord Balmoral was in evidence, of course, since his Bagatelle Club team were the challengers. I nodded to Lady Windemere and the duchess of Paisley, present with their usual entourage, and exchanged pleasantries with Baroness Jeurdon and Lady Lind-Mead.

When the competition finally got under way, I was at a bit of a loss to understand how they managed the whole thing. There were a number of events, and the paper targets, with circled bull's-eyes, were gradually moved farther and farther from the riflemen. There was much measuring of distances from bullet hole to target center, and the endeavors of various contestants were accompanied by suitable *ooohs* and *ahhhs*. If asked point-blank, I would have stated that they seemed to be making a mountain out of a molehill. Then I noted the exchange of currency between top-hatted gentlemen and realized that the number of matches was to accommodate the spectators urge to wager.

The shooting took place in a sizeable fenced area at the rear of the Wellington Club building. Chairs were arranged on the brick-paved terrace, and the back wall was sandbagged to a considerable height. Due to the position of the property in conjunction with the Deptford Reach, there were no buildings immediately adjacent and a fortuitous breeze off the river served to disperse the fumes of the gun powder. With a gay crowd sipping tea or other more potent libations, and the marksmen in uniforms of paramilitary design banging away at targets, it made for a colorful scene. Holmes seemed to understand what was going on and informed me that the results of the match now depended on the final encounter between the ace of the Bagatelle Club, one Gerald Stolte, and our acquaintance Richard Ledger.

The groundswell of conversation interspersed with tinkles of laughter faded out as the two contestants made for their firing positions. Lord Arthur Seville was acting as an announcer, and he informed the multitude that this would be the penultimate event, since the victor would then entertain his audience with an individual display. This deciding match would be five shots per contestant with no time limit. A two-by-four timber was placed on the ground to serve as the marker for the shootists, they being allowed to change position as long as they remained behind the length of wood.

Holmes and I were standing at the rear of the seated crowd, on the four steps leading from the clubhouse to the terrace and the rifle range beyond. A well-dressed though somewhat sly-looking citizen standing next to me advanced some inside news for no reason that I could fathom.

"That bit about changing positions was introduced into the procedural rules by Chasseur, you can bet," he whispered to me.

I noted an oversized diamond on one of his fingers that struck me as gauche, though I judged the gem to be real. My questioning look prompted him to continue in a conspiratorial tone.

"Chasseur has more than a few bob wagered on this contest, and Ledger is his hole card." My eyebrows must have escalated, for he elaborated. "His sleeve ace, but the bloke is a nervous type, as you shall shortly see."

As though in fear that he had been too revealing, my unknown ally changed his position. I found out later from Holmes that he was Odds On Olderman, London's leading bookmaker, though he was surely present under an alias.

Representing the challengers, Gerald Stolte was first to take position and proved to be a testbook marksman, as immobile as a block of stone. Once positioned in a widespread stance, with the butt of

the stock against his shoulder, he might as well
have been a statue. I noted that his right thumb
was not curved over the throat of the butt but
rested parallel to the barrell, close to the bolt of the
army-issue rifle he was using. His right eye glued to
the rear sight, he remained stationary for a nerve-
racking time before loosing his first shot. I could
barely see the target, but Stolte obviously could,
and the bull's-eye as well. He did not move other
than a quick back and forth of the bolt with his
thumb and index finger. Then, with a gentle caress
of the trigger, he sent off his second shot. With the
same approximate period between, his final three
bullets spun down the barrel's rifling and boomed
their way to the target.

With no expression on his face, Stolte lowered his
weapon and retreated toward a group of his Bagatelle teammates, to discuss his efforts no doubt. A
club attendant raced out to retrieve the target,
bringing it to Lord Arthur Seville after affixing a
new one.

I must say the large gathering was suitably quiet,
and I felt caught up by the suspense myself. Seville
inspected the target, conferred with two other
gentlemen, and then made an announcement.

"Mr. Stolte's five shots were all within the inner
three rings, and two are judged to be bull's-eyes."

There were cheers from the Bagatelle Club supporters and I noted Alvidon Chasseur, standing
with a group of men, looking confident, nay somewhat smug.

When Richard Ledger advanced to the shooting
position, I was surprised to see that he carried a
lever-action rifle loosely in his hand. I would have
thought that the contestants would use similar
pieces of ordinance, but some words between two
men slightly to our rear informed me that the

marksmen had their choice of guns, providing the caliber was within the specified limits allowed.

Whereas Stolte had been pedantic in his actions, Richard Ledger was not, and his style was as far from that of his opponent as could be imagined. He stood with his gun held in his right hand, barrel to the sky, surveying the target. Then he ran his left thumb across his mouth and passed that finger across the front sight, lowering the barrel to make this action possible. Suddenly the butt was against his shoulder and he fired almost without pause. His right hand levered the empty cartridge from the firing chamber as his legs moved him a step or two to his right and he got off another quick shot. Then his stance shifted to his left and the next three bullets were fired in rapid succession as Ledger continued to change position.

Throughout the crowd there was an exchange of looks and shrugs, and I surmised that most of those present could not quite believe the marksman's unusual methods. There were some who did not register surprise, Chasseur among them, and I judged that Ledger's unorthodox approach was normal to him. The crowd obviously felt that Stolte had triumphed for the Bagatelle Club, since the Wellington man, because of his speed, had seemed not to care about the result and had almost given the impression that he was throwing the match.

With the thought that the result was obvious, small talk started up again, but when the target was brought to Lord Seville, there was something about his manner and that of the two other judges that stilled eager tongues. Finally, Seville addressed the gathering.

"Mr. Ledger's target has no bull's-eye, since it has been blown away. The Wellington Club retains its championship of the London Rifle League."

His lordship's words were greeted by a stunned silence, and then a series of cheers arose from the amazed gallery and there was a babble of sound. It took Seville some time to quiet the spectators, which he finally did by removing his topper and waving it as an attention getter.

"Now, ladies and gentlemen, Mr. Ledger will give a demonstration of trick shooting as the final event of the day."

His skill a recognized thing, the audience was riveted on the champion and there was a respectful silence indeed.

As he took his stance before the crowd, I was much surprised to note that he had changed weapons. Having done so well with his lever-action gun, I would have thought that he would stay with it; but instead, he now carried a different looking rifle, with an elongated barrel. It was an unusual weapon with a stock decorated by ornate checkering. I had seen similar carving on sporting rifles and understood it had a grip-aiding purpose.

"Note that he is using a Beals revolving rifle," whispered Holmes in my ear. "They haven't made those since 'seventy-two."

While I mused over this information, Ledger put on a show that had the crowd breathless. Lord Seville stood to one side of the marksman with another judge, and both men alternated in spinning coins into the air. Ledger knocked four out of the sky and then added a filip by drilling two more, firing from the hip. As he paused to reload, I realized why his repeating rifle had seemed strange. Its firing chamber was similar to a revolver in its action, hence the name that Holmes had given the gun.

While I watched open-mouthed as Ledger ran through his bag of trick-shooting feats, a thought came to my mind, spurred by the fact that the man and his gun moved as one. It was further stimulated by his speed in firing and the so brief time that he took to aim.

The climax to Ledger's performance should have been clear to me before the fact. The afternoon had been a singular triumph for Alvidon Chasseur, and if I judged him correctly, he must have derived great joy from forcing Lord Balmoral to take a back seat. Would he let the matter come to an end without interjecting himself into the proceedings? Certainly not; though I had to admit that he displayed remarkable nerve in the manner in which he did it.

Ledger now completed what proved to be his next to closing bit of rifle legerdemain. With his weapon held by Lord Seville, he faced the audience, two small wooden balls in hand. Tossing them over his shoulder, he snatched the Beals repeater from his lordship's hands and whirled, again firing from the hip, and smashed his targets with twin shots that rang out almost as one. As he acknowledged the applause, a look passed between the president of the Birmingham and Northern and Ledger. The marksman reloaded his weapon as Chasseur, without an announcement, strode out onto the firing range. From a silver case he extracted a cigarette as a puzzled hush spread over the crowd. Igniting an Egyptian cigarette, which I identified from its length, the rail tycoon stood with his profile toward Ledger, the smoking cigarette in his mouth. By now everyone realized what was going on, and there was a low rumble of protest and several of the ladies present grew quite pale. I have mentioned that the cigarette was long, and I noted that Chasseur held it between his teeth at the very end; but still, it was a sporty exhibition of faith in his employee's ability.

Ledger did take time aiming now. Then the shot rang out and the burning end of the cigarette was no more as Chasseur turned toward the audience with a triumphant smile. He rejoined the excited throng to the tune of hearty cheers, this time as much for him as for Ledger.

Holmes was exhibiting a sardonic smile. "The old reprobate carried it off like a circus ringmaster," he stated.

"It was an impressive piece of showmanship, Holmes."

"I'll not say you nay on that. Has a thought been nagging at you?"

"The candle in our sitting room?"

"Exactly. I don't think Ledger would have missed the wick."

I agreed quickly. Actually, that was not the thought that had come to my mind at all.

Chapter 13

❧

Watson's Investigation, Holmes's Revelations

THROUGH THE mass of spectators, all now standing and discussing the happenings, I noted Claymore Frisbee making his way purposefully in our direction. Some sort of conference with the banker was overdue, and I could add little to it. So I took a bold step and spoke to Holmes hurriedly.

"I have an idea. Would it be inconvenient if I took this time to pursue it?"

"By no means," responded my friend. There was a faint twinkle in his intense eyes and he cocked his head slightly, surveying me. "You know my methods, Watson. Do make use of them. In conjunction with your talents, of course."

"Now see here, Holmes . . ."

"I'm serious. If you're on the scent of something, by all means have at it. I'll see you later at Baker Street."

Holmes turned to wave a greeting at the approaching Frisbee, then returned his attention to me.

"Good hunting, old friend."

Well, I thought as I made my way inside the

clubhouse, you've stuck your neck out this time, Watson. Things will get sticky if you botch it, so have your wits about you.

A solicitous club attendant readily gave me the information I requested and shortly thereafter I found myself in the basement of the club, outside a small room which I had been informed was given over to the star performer of the Wellington gun squad.

Richard Ledger was already within, having removed himself from his many admirers promptly. But then it was Alvidon Chasseur who was taking the bows, a pleasure he had paid for; and I judged that he paid Ledger well.

The marksman recognized me immediately and invited me to enter his dressing room. Trying to emulate Holmes, I bid my eyes make note of the surroundings, hoping to implant them upon a mental photographic plate. It was a small place, partitioned off like numerous others for the convenience of club members, which Ledger certainly was, though it was not his money paying the dues. There was a locker for hanging clothes, since the rifle squad affected costumes bearing the Wellington insignia. A cupboard was the largest piece of furniture, the top section being a rack for rifles with glass doors secured by an efficient-looking lock. A drawer underneath was closed and also sported a lock. I suspected that it contained an assortment of small arms.

On a square table there were tools, and I noted a bullet mold and a small but serviceable looking vise, which gave me a thought.

"For half loads?" I asked, indicating the equipment.

"Sometimes handy," admitted Ledger. He was

slipping into his suit coat and shot a sudden look at me as though making up his mind.

"You see how it is, Doctor. There's not just the shooting involved."

"A bit of a side show as well," I hazarded.

The man's pale blue eyes were disconcerting, but if one overlooked them, his manner was forthright and friendly. Evidently, he sensed a kindred spirit in me.

"I have to be ready to change the act, you see. If it's not long guns, there's naught left but sidearms and for fancy work, half loads are helpful."

"Less recoil for greater accuracy."

The fact that I understood seemed to please him.

"Tricks of the trade." He shifted subjects. "Can you talk about the treasure train matter?"

His directness was refreshing. Leaning against the table, he seemed relaxed; but I knew I was in the presence of a coiled spring. The man reflected his profession: dangerous, certainly ruthless if necessary, but his youth dissipated any suggestion of malevolence. I will grant that I rank with the gullible, certainly in comparison to Holmes. Yet I felt that Ledger was sincere, his mood tinged by a genuine regret—not for his performance of the day, but relative to the matter of the stolen gold.

I decided to take a chance. My companion of so many years had once said that to learn something one should tell something, so I became revealing.

"Sherlock Holmes seems intrigued by this gun club competition that has sprung up."

"The trained seals." There was a twist to Ledger's mouth. "I shouldn't complain, for it's what got me my job with the railroad; and marksmanship competition is nothing new. The other stuff, like the cigarette bit, is just so much lagniappe to entertain the people."

I must have been regarding him rather intently, for he shifted position, possibly a nervous movement, and was now seated on the table.

"Does Mr. Holmes associate the Wellington Club with the robbery?"

I shook my head promptly. "There's quite a few gun clubs. Holmes is looking for a lead as to who actually pulled off the robbery. The soldiers in the field, as 'twere."

This struck a chord within Ledger.

"Now I see it. Ex-military working for business firms, meeting people at the clubs; they could have caught wind of the treasure train." Suddenly he shook his head. "From what I've heard of Mr. Holmes, he's not one for just theorizing. There must be something more."

I decided to plunge in deeper. "A shot was fired at our sitting room. Holmes contends that it was not an assassination attempt, but it had to be done by a sharpshooter."

Those light blue eyes remained devoid of emotion, though a slight smile curled Ledger's lips. "That puts me in the front ranks, I suppose?"

"I think not. Besides, it was a long shot. I doubt if that Beals revolving rifle you fancy could have carried far enough."

He was not offended. "You noticed that did you, Doctor?" Ledger became silent, and I sensed he was considering a thought. Then he continued: "If there's some marksman playing games, it does point a finger at the gun clubs. Does Mr. Holmes know how the robbery was executed?"

I decided not to carry my revelations too far. "I've a thought that he's got a pretty good idea." Had I said no, it would have been an insult to Holmes, and Ledger wouldn't have believed me anyway.

"I haven't. Don't feel good about it either. If I'd done my job right . . ." His voice dwindled away, and then he rose from his half-seated position. "Would there be something that I could do, Doctor?"

"You could consider Holmes's idea about your marksman colleagues," I replied with an authoritative tone that startled me.

"I will," he said.

That was the end of our meeting but not of my investigations.

The waning sun had dropped below the horizon, leaving a momentary afterglow as I alighted from a hansom at 221 B Baker Street.

As I entered the sitting room, the sleuth was seated at his desk, its surface cluttered with cables and penned notations. Not the cold, thinking machine, he, but more the general, assaying reports from the front. He seemed pleased, for he slapped the desktop with an open palm and exhibited a wide smile.

"By George, Watson, I was wagering on you, and from your appearance, I know that victory has graced your banners."

"I do think I've stumbled onto something, Holmes."

"About Ledger, of course."

Being in the process of removing my greatcoat, I almost dropped it in surprise.

"A trip to the Wellington Club competition sparks you into action. Who was there connected with the treasure train matter? Alvidon Chasseur and Claymore Frisbee, but we can dismiss both, for there was nothing revelatory regarding them. We have left Richard Ledger, whose prowess with firearms astonished even me."

"It was his manner, you see."

"Capital, Watson. It prompted you to suspect that the deadly marksman is an imposter and not Richard Ledger, formerly of the army of India, at all."

The froth of my manner was frostbitten by reality. Confound it, I could never get ahead of the man. As I lowered myself into the cane-bottom Restoration chair, my sudden despondency had to be apparent and Holmes seized upon it.

"Come now, my stab at the truth was ill-conceived, for I do not know that for a fact and suspect that you do. Relate the path that your investigation followed."

I made a weary gesture with one hand. "What use? You already know."

"Suspect. A far cry from know. A report, good Watson, if you please."

I knew that I was not being twitted. Holmes's expression was as contrite as an erring schoolboy's, so I rallied some enthusiasm and plunged into my tale.

"The man's style led me to the conclusion that rifles were not his métier."

Holmes registered enthusiasm. "Here your superior knowledge of firearms comes into play."

Remembering his identification of the Beals rifle, I did not choose to accept this remark in whole but continued.

"Recall how the chap moved while shooting, not choosing to stay positioned as the other marksmen did?"

There were wrinkles on Holmes's broad brow. "It was unusual, though I drew no conclusions from it."

"He's used to shooting at moving targets."

"Since the target was stationary, he moved to compensate. How clever of you."

I regarded him warily. "You were already suspicious of the man. Holmes, if you are leading me on . . ."

"I assure you that is furthest from my mind. I did not take note of the point you are making." Holmes paused as though wondering why, then concluded. "Possibly for reasons I will relate in a moment. Tell all, good chap."

"Ledger, for want of a better name, is really a small-arms expert. Gunfighter is the word that comes to mind."

"American, then?"

"Oh yes," I replied airily. "The speed with which he fired, his frequent shooting from the hip, his use of the Beals revolving rifle, which is constructed like a hand gun—it all smacked of one from the American West. Southwest, I would guess."

"How so?" Perhaps he was just trying to encourage me, but Holmes seemed captivated.

"I spoke with the man."

My friend nodded. "That I assumed."

"He made use of the word *lagniappe*." Since Holmes was regarding me with a questioning look, I continued, not without some pride I might add.

"It's a colloquialism of the southern part of the United States. Refers to a gratuitous additive, like baker's dozen."

"Excellent, excellent."

"In his dressing room at the club I noted some tools, and upon questioning, the chap told me he intended to use half loads for some hand gun exhibitions."

Holmes merely shook his head, and I might have detected an expression of amazement in his eyes. Or was it pride?

"Another American innovation. Trick shooting with a hand gun seldom requires range; and the targets are small, so there is little need for great force at impact. Professionals reduce the powder charge in the bullets, which in turn lessens the recoil at firing and increases the accuracy of the man behind the gun."

Holmes burst out in a peal of laughter, most unusual for him. "Beekeeping on the Sussex Downs moves ever closer in my future plans as you talk, old friend. Will you allow me to take Mrs. Hudson with me?"

"Be serious."

He suppressed his merriment. "You've done a splendid job. Now we but need conclusive proof."

"We have it." I must say his reaction to my coup-de-maître was most gratifying.

"I've spent a good part of the afternoon with our former client General Sternways. While, out of courtesy, consuming more of his port than I fancy, I learned that the general knew of Ledger. He commented that the man was indeed a splendid shot despite the fact that a boyhood accident had cost him the third and fourth fingers of his left hand."

"That's it, then!" Holmes sprang from his chair and began pacing the room, unconsciously following the path that I knew so well. "As to the whereabouts of the true Richard Ledger, we know not; but this chap is a proven imposter," he stated in that removed tone as though speaking to himself. "We can assume that the fellow is an American, though I must say he passes himself off quite well as British. Therefore, I deduce that he's spent some time in England or knew the real Ledger well. But how does this aid us? To use an expression of the western United States that you are so well versed in, Watson, we've cast a wide loop in this case. It is time we began to tighten the noose."

"Just a moment, Holmes. Before we dwell on other matters, what was it that alerted you to the possibility of a masquerader? Also, you fall very easily into the assumption—unproven—that he is American."

Holmes ceased his pacing to stand by the bookshelf, his left hand outstretched to finger, unconsciously, the golden statue on the fourth shelf that was a memento of a previous case.

"The plan to defend the treasure train. It was good, but decidedly un-British."

"You know I can't follow that."

"Space is the clue. From London to Great Yarmouth, a train passes through a stream of stations and steams by countless habitations. In the American West, the rails stretch for hundreds of miles without encountering a village or inhabitant, for that matter, save grazing bison.* The best means of guarding the gold here in England would have been to place some stout lads, well armed, within the boxcar, for surely they could defend it until the sound of a battle brought reinforcements. In America, or at least the western part, it is a different story. Once the robbers gain control of the train, they have adequate time to force entry, for aid is far removed and the noise of a conflict is wasted on the desert air."

"Of course," I exclaimed. "The armored guardhouse being designed to protect the engine as well as the cargo. To keep the train moving."

Satisfied on this point, I fell silent and allowed Holmes to resume his thoughtful pacing. After a period, he came to a standstill by the mantle and reached for his cherrywood but thought the better

---

*It is interesting to note that Holmes professed but a vague knowledge of western America yet, quite correctly did not refer to buffalo.

of it. Instead, he went to the coal skuttle and removed a cigar from that most singular humidor.

"All right, Watson, let us beat the wheat from the chaff, for it is nigh on to harvest time or better be." Through a cloud of aromatic smoke he became more specific. "Claymore Frisbee informed me today that there is pressure on Inter-Ocean to pay the insurance claim. Chasseur is off to Cornwall for a stockholders' meeting but wants to deal with the matter directly upon his return." He paused, considering a new question. "Why Cornwall? His principal backers are a cadre of Scottish financiers. No matter. A cable from our friend Von Shalloway informs me that the Deutsch Bank is negotiating a deal regarding four hundred thousand pounds' worth of gold."

"How does that fit in?"

"*Mehr Licht*! More light. Goethe's last words are apropos to the fine art of deduction."

"Never mind Goethe. I'm confused."

"Fortunately, I am not. Mainly because of your fortuitous remark."

I grunted. "That's the second time you've made reference to something I said, Holmes, and I'm dashed if I know what it was."

"Your exact words were: 'You have established a possible connection between Michael and Ezariah Trelawney.'"

"Both Ramsey Michael and Ezeriah Trelawney are dead, and I don't see what was revealing about my words."

"It was the sound. We have three principals in this plot at the moment, and there is something unusual about their names: Michael, Ezariah, and Hananish."

"The latter not only being alive but up to his neck in the affair."

"Exactly. Cast your mind back to Bible classes, Watson. Were there not three wise men in Babylon? Shadrach, Meshach, and Abednego."

"Shadrach," I exclaimed. "The code word used by the man who killed Ramsey Michael."

"Exactly. But the three ancients were brought to Babylon from the land of Israel, where their names were Hananiah, Mishael, and Azariah."

I just stared at Holmes, wide-eyed.

"Ezariah Trelawney, Ramsey Michael, and Burton Hananish all served in the Crimea. They were in the same regiment and received honorable mention in dispatches from Balaklava and Sevastopol. Three men whose names are so close to three biblical figures had to strike up an acquaintance. I now deal in theory, but there is so much corroboration that it might as well be fact. I envision a close friendship, which continued into civilian life. A foray into the byways of the larcenious could have been suggested by the matter of the French gold, though I suspect they involved themselves in conspiracies prior to the treasure train. Remember that Michael had some hidden source of income. I think he uncovered the Credit Lyonnais matter, bringing it to the attention of his banking cohorts. They secured the gold, and Michael probably recruited the bully boys who did the deed."

"Who engineered it? Not three old men, surely?"

"All with military experience, remember." I sensed that Holmes did not find this too palatable, but another thought then came to my mind.

"When the assassin went to Michael's house and used the name Shadrach to gain admittance . . ."

"The art critic assumed he carried a message from Hananish. In the Bible, Hananiah became Shadrach."

"Then Hananish hired this Lightfoot chap to kill off his partners."

"The cripple is the only one of the trio still alive, so that statement seems to have merit," replied Holmes dryly.

"But if they were close friends? . . ."

"I mentioned but recently that thieves fall out. Possibly Hananish felt that his co-conspirators had served their purpose and were best out of the way. Or, and I rather fancy this idea, Hananish is going for even bigger game and wants to clear his back trail."

I was incapable of following this line of reasoning and did not question Holmes about it, since there was an interruption in our discussion. A tap on the door and Billy presented himself with an envelope, which he handed to Holmes, along with some news.

"A gentleman's below askin' fer you, Mr. 'Olmes. Ledger by name."

A quick look flashed between the sleuth and myself as he signaled for Billy to show the gun expert up.

"Quick dividends on your investigation, Watson."

"I hope so."

Then Ledger was at our door. It was Holmes who ushered him in. After disposing of his coat, the youthful-looking chap came to the point with a promptness that must have sat well with my friend.

"Dr. Watson told me about a shot fired at you, sir," he said.

"More in the general vicinity, I think," responded the sleuth.

"Could you show me roughly the path of the bullet?" he asked.

Holmes indicated the windowpane through

which the missle had passed. He then showed Ledger where the spent bullet had lodged itself in our floorboards. The man plotted the flight of the slug much as Holmes had done, and then gazed out at the night scene. After letting his eyes wander for a moment, he indicated a building, standing tall in the next block, to Holmes and myself, who were now beside him at the bow window.

"What might that be?" he inquired.

"The warehouse of Spears and Henry, the well-known liquor firm. The answer to your next question is yes. A man could have gained the roof without much difficulty and escaped from the area rapidly as well."

"That's the spot," stated Ledger. "It's a goodly distance, but a Sharps rifle could have made it."

Another quick glance passed between Holmes and myself. The sleuth knew that the Sharps was an American make, and he promptly proved it.

"It was a small bullet that I extracted from the floorboards."

"A Mauser, then," said Ledger. "The Germans are manufacturing them in quantity. A long-range high-velocity small-bore rifle using smokeless powder. Selling them to the Boers in Africa. There'll be some trouble down there one of these days."* Noting surprise on both our faces, he explained. "Mercenaries are rather tuned to such matters, you see."

"I do," replied Holmes. "What is your thought regarding the shot? I'd better tell you that I think it was fired at a candle that was on the desk there." He indicated the spot he was referring to.

"Did he hit the candle?" asked Ledger quickly.

---

*The masquerader called the turn here, for the Boer War broke out in 1899, and the British cavalry was decimated by the very weapon he described in the hands of master marksmen.

At Holmes's nod, a sigh escaped the man. "That helps, sir, for there's just so many that good."

"Could you have done it?" inquired Holmes.

For a split second there was a flashing smile of almost boyish bravado on our visitor's face. "If the other light in the room was dim, the candle would have stood out nicely. I think I could have hit the wick."

"So do I," replied Holmes, "and that's what I think our unknown shootist was aiming at."

It was obvious that Ledger appreciated the word *unknown*.

"It gives me an idea of where to look. The doctor here said you thought some of the hired sharp-shooters were involved."

"You might consider the name of Ramsey Michael."

"That art critic chap who was murdered?"

"I'd be interested to know if any of the marksmen were ever approached by him."

"All right, Mr. Holmes." The pseudo-Ledger was no waster of words and took his departure at this point.

I was regarding Holmes with some concern. "What if the chap was involved in the robbery?"

"A possibility."

"Aren't you rather setting yourself up as a target?"

"We've been that for some time, Watson—both of us, if you will recall."

Holmes had taken the lamp from the small Duncan Phyfe table near the bow window and passed it across the panes of glass once. Replacing it, he caught me regarding him with amazement.

"I don't want Ledger detained by Burlington Bertie or Tiny, you see. The American just might be able to do us a considerable service."

Of course, I thought. He's got the premises staked out. Probably with arrangements to follow visitors if need be, which means the involvement of Slippery Styles, the human shadow. No wonder Holmes was so casual about a possible attempt on us. Though unseen, the boys from Limehouse were on duty.

As I dwelled on this comforting fact, Holmes had seated himself at the desk and opened the message delivered by Billy at the time that the American had arrived. Now his eyes rose from the single sheet of foolscap.

"Most interesting. I sent Billy to the Diogenes Club with some questions for Mycroft. He provided a record of recent gold transactions for us, you recall."

The sleuth's thin and dexterous fingers indicated the message before him. "My brother assures me that Burton Hananish has not been involved in the sale of precious metal up to this time."

"You suspected that he had been?"

"When something works, there is a natural inclination to repeat it. With two bankers involved, I had a thought that the treasure train matter might be a sequel to a previous manipulation, sporting new trappings, of course."

"But, Holmes, there have been no big bullion robberies in recent years. I read the papers, too."

"Granted. But some family plate, old coins purloined from a collection, some dentures, and given the necessary equipment and expertise, it can all be melted down. Remove the alloy and you have pure gold, which can be poured into molds and—presto—gold bullion, as valuable as that taken from the treasure train."

Here was a new thought, and my mind raced to grasp it.

"You picture a large-scale fencing operation to dispose of stolen gold by converting objects into metal."

"With the necessary purification. Gold is quite unique, Watson. Say you have a medallion of twenty-four-carat gold . . ."

"I wouldn't mind, really."

"Alas, we deal but in fantasy. Your medallion is beautifully engraved and valuable, but it is stolen. Being identifiable, the thief would be well advised to melt it down, for without its engraving and shaping, the object is still of value for it is pure gold."

"Your point being that my medallion could completely lose its identity without losing all its value."

"Which is more than can be said for precious jewels or rare paintings. But we wander far afield. I am dropping the fence idea and am now considering another more to the point."

Again Holmes tapped the letter on the desk.

"My brother touches on a matter relative to the cable from Von Shalloway."

"I wondered when you would bring that up. What has the esteemed chief of the Berlin police to do with this case?"

"He is our fastest and most accurate contact in mid-Europe. There are many twists and turns to this matter, Watson, but one fact stands out. We went to Gloucester to approach Hananish. I wished to see the man and size him up. In our interview, little was said that was not old hat. Yet shortly thereafter a dirty tricks brigade attempted to spirit you away with the idea of laying me by the heels as well. If Hananish was behind it, something must have been said that got his hackles up. I believe it was his inadvertent reference to the Deutsch Bank."

"That's why you contacted Von Shalloway in Berlin."

"With good results. But let us deal with this in a step progression. One: the gold bonds of the Credit Lyonnais can be redeemed by the investors in two weeks, two: the five hundred thousand pounds' worth of gold on the treasure train has been stolen and, as of this moment, not recovered; three: according to von Shalloway, the Deutsch Bank has made an arrangement with the Bank of England . . ."

"Bank of England! What have they to do with this?"

Holmes admonished me with a waving forefinger.

"Hear me out, Watson. The Deutsch Bank has arranged an option whereby they can purchase within the next ten days four hundred thousand pounds' worth of gold bullion now in the vaults of the Bank of England. The gold is registered in the name of Burton Hananish."

"I have it now," I exclaimed. "The Bank of England is acting as a clearing house for Hananish."

"Correct."

"And the Credit Lyonnais is, in effect, taking out insurance. In case Scotland Yard or Sherlock Holmes doesn't locate the stolen gold, they've made a deal with the Deutsch Bank to fulfill their needs."

"Your grasp of the situation is admirable, Watson. Of course the French made inquiries in banking circles as to the availability of the amount of gold they needed the moment the treasure train was robbed. What more natural that they should contact the Deutsch Bank? The two nations make a habit of snarling at each other but continue to do business much like the Greeks and the Turks. But doesn't it strike you that Hananish could have contacted the Credit Lyonnais directly?"

I decided to fly the white flag rather than try to piece together the point Holmes was making.

"I'm becoming hopelessly mired. You have introduced major banks of three nations, along with two west coast bankers, and there is more backing and filling relative to this whole thing than I can cope with."

"Exactly the idea, Watson. Hananish is playing the obstructionist, muddying his back trail. You mentioned the possibility of Scotland Yard or Sherlock Holmes locating the stolen gold. Sherlock Holmes has located it, or a major portion of it. It rests in the vaults of the Bank of England, registered to Hananish."

This was something I could understand and I indicated as much.

Holmes continued: "When we cut through the extraneous, the evidence is sufficient for a presumption of fact. Hananish, with no previous record of dealing in gold, is part of a consortium of west coast banks in the Credit Lyonnais deal. The gold is stolen and he deposits an almost equal sum in the Bank of England under his name. No mention of other banks now."

"Why, it's open and shut."

"So our friend at the Red Grouse in Fenley said."

"Then you intend to move against Hananish?"

"Not right now. There is a little pressure of time, but there are still a few stray threads to be unraveled. How did the robbers get the gold from Brent, in Essex, to the Bank of England? As knowledgeable a fellow as Dandy Jack the smuggler couldn't tell us."

"There is that," I admitted.

"Also the thought that the trio of conspirators, Hananish, Trelawney, and Michael, may have been up to some previous mischief. I'd like to cast light on that possibility."

"Reasonable," I agreed, as though my opinion really mattered.

"Then there is the presence of Lightfoot, which does not rest easy with me."

"It does with me." Holmes registered some surprise at my strong stand. "Hananish used this notorious assassin to wipe out his co-conspirators. To further muddy his trail, for they cannot peach on him now. I would think that he's set the man after you."

Holmes startled me by seeming to accept this in part.

"Hananish did say that he had read those romanticized case histories you make available, on occasion, to the reading public. He must know of my . . . er . . . our excellent connections in Berlin."

I interrupted, excitedly. "Surely he is in fear of exactly what has happened—your ferreting out the Credit Lyonnais-Deutsch Bank-Bank of England arrangement, which leads right back to him."

As Holmes mused on this, I added with conviction, "I'm jolly glad that Burlington Bertie and Tiny are on the job. Where have you got them tucked away?"

"In Professor vonKrugg's house next door," replied Holmes, his mind elsewhere. I smiled at this, for Holmes was Professor vonKrugg, the seldom-seen language expert.

"Slippery Styles is staked out in the empty house across the street," added my friend.

"Good show, Holmes. For once you are taking precautions regarding your safety."

"And yours, old fellow," he said, rising to his feet.

I felt a stab of emotion, for he consistently tried to do that.

Holmes was standing by the desk, looking down at the letter from his brother.

"Mycroft added a postscript to this which is intriguing: 'Am, of a sudden, interested in your investigation relative to the Deutsch Bank. Please keep me informed.'"

His eyes swiveled up to meet mine. "Now what has gotten the wind up with Mycroft relative to the German banking institution?"

"I certainly don't know, but we've gone around and around on this matter and there are a couple of points you can clear up."

Holmes crossed to the mantle in search of a pipe. "I'm at your service."

"About Ledger. He's an imposter. What are you going to do about it?"

"I really don't know. If he's sincere in lending aid, he's much better situated to investigate the hired marksmen than we are. As regards his assuming the identity of Richard Ledger, I'm not at all sure that has any connection with the train robbery."

I allowed the matter to rest there and pursued another thought that had been tantalizing me.

"It is past history, Holmes, but how did you show up so opportunely on that river tug?"

My friend smiled. "As though by divine providence? But think a moment, Watson, and all is clear. You are spirited away on the river road leaving an obvious trail, which Orloff promptly picked up. On my return to the Red Grouse Inn I learned what Orloff had and, in addition, that he was in hot pursuit. With the thought that he could handle anything that came his way, I chose to survey the area by water. Your captors might have tried to spirit you away via the river, you know?"

Finally satisfied on this point, I found myself suddenly at a loss for words. Holmes sensed my mood.

"Come aloft,* Watson," he cried. "A good dinner, a bottle of wine, and conversation removed from this business at hand. 'Twill lead to clear minds for the busy times ahead."

---

*An unusual expression for Holmes. Of naval origin and meaning "Let's enjoy ourselves." The great detective does use it in conjunction with a bottle of wine, and the expression is thought to have been associated with "high with wine," though it is doubtful that Holmes was suggesting that he and his confrere get stoned.

Chapter 14

❧

The Unanticipated Fact

WHEN I descended from my bedchamber the following morning, I found Holmes at breakfast and in good spirits. He waved a cablegram at me as I poured my coffee.

"I was about to call you, good fellow, for we will have visitors shortly."

"Not that Lightfoot, I trust," I mumbled, pouring thick Devonshire cream into my cup.

"There is no report on Moriarty's former henchman, but Orloff will be with us, along with our ally in Fenley."

I had not as yet sampled my morning eye opener, which was unfortunate. "Wallingford?" I exclaimed, and could have bit my lips in vexation, for I had let the cat out for fair.

Holmes was way ahead of me. "Do not be concerned, Watson. During our last meeting at the Red Grouse, you treated the man's words with unusual deference and I deduced that you knew his true identity."

"Holmes, I did not mean to pry . . ." I began, shamefaced.

"Tut, tut. You must have found out from Orloff, for he is the only one involved that knows. Anyone who can extract information from our security agent friend does not deserve censure from me, but rather warrants admiration."

Considerably buoyed by these words, I attacked my morning meal with gusto. Holmes did provide a codicil to his sporting statement.

"For his peace of mind, let us not refer to Mr. Wallingford by his name."

"I understand," I replied, munching on one of Mrs. Hudson's really superior scones.

It was shortly after the vestiges of our breakfast were cleared away that the security agent and the former confidence man arrived.

To my surprise I learned that they had come from Shaw. I had assumed that they both arrived on our doorstep from Gloucester, but the reasons became obvious as the meeting of minds progressed.

The American was as buoyant as the last time I had seen him, and he obviously felt that his labors had born fruit.

"I think I've got it, Mr. Holmes. How it all started, I mean. Your suggestion that I run a parallel investigation on Ezariah Trelawney was what gave me the key. Also that constable, Bennett by name, took your cable to heart and opened a lot of doors for me."

"Good man," commented Holmes.

"Trelawney, after his army service, returned to Shaw and went to work at the bank. He was good at his job. Shaw is a small place, and his advancement was rapid. Now the bank made a practice of keeping a supply of gold on hand. It dated back to the Napoleonic wars. They had to get a courier to Stockholm, Sweden, and it was at that time that a false rumor spread over England that the French fleet had triumphed at Trafalgar and Nelson had been defeated. There was widespread panic. In times like that, paper doesn't talk. The Shaw Bank did not have sufficient gold available to tempt a merchant skipper to carry their man to Sweden, and whatever the deal was, it fell through. So a policy was established to have a certain amount of gold, sovereigns or whatever, on hand at all times. Modern business methods antiquated this idea, but it had produced a favorable climate with depositors. Shaw is an agrarian area, and people close to the land tend to think in basics. Floods, frosts, pestilence, and the like. The fact that the Shaw Bank kept gold in its vaults led to its gaining a considerable reputation as being sound and conservative."

Wallingford paused in his report and a smile crossed his face. "You know, the old gold brick dodge always worked in the sticks . . ." He caught himself and affected a cough to cover his embarrassment at this revelation.

"Anyway, the gold-in-reserve idea became rather a trademark of Trelawney's bank, and it spread to other west coast banks as well."

"Explaining how they happened to readily have a surplus of the precious metal," said Holmes. He had indicated no impatience at Wallingford's detailed recounting, and I sensed that he was much interested in the complete picture of the Trelawney-Hananish operation.

"Hananish returned to Gloucester after being mustered out, and he was more fortunate in that his father was president of the bank there and he rather inherited the position."

Holmes, his eyes on the ceiling, suddenly shot Wallingford a sharp glance, which the man interpreted.

"Both Hananish's bank and the one in Shaw were publicly owned, each by a small group of stockholders."

Holmes's gaze retreated, again, to the ceiling.

"The gold reserve in both banks was annually listed as part of the assets, but most of the time it wasn't there at all."

Holmes leaned forward in his chair suddenly, and Wallingford certainly had my attention as well. Orloff, already privy to the information, was blowing smoke rings.

"Under the banking laws, there are spot checks by examiners; but Trelawney was prepared for this, Hananish as well. If there was official inquiry as to the whereabouts of the reserve gold, Trelawney had at hand a letter of credit from Hananish's bank for the amount of the gold plus the date that the metal would be returned and the agreement whereby Trelawney had made the gold temporarily available to Hananish."

Holmes rose to his feet, now restless with anticipation.

"But these agreements never passed through the normal channels of either bank."

"Nor were the stockholders informed, nor was there interest charged," responded Wallingford.

I could not supress a question at this point.

"Where was the gold, then?"

Wallingford shrugged. "That I could not learn. This embraces a matter of some years, you understand. All that time what was supposed to be a reserve fund was actually in movement: being invested, acting as collateral, who knows what."

Holmes, standing by the bow window with his back to the group, suddenly whirled around.

"I expressed a desire to look into previous mischief of Hananish and Trelawney—Michael as well.

You recall, Watson? This information should provide a fruitful lead as well as something to throw at Hananish when we close in on him."

Orloff was snubbing out one of the small, black cigars he fancied. "Are you prepared to make your move?"

Holmes crossed to the mantelpiece, assuming a familiar position beside it. Ah hah, I thought. He's ready for the denouement.

The sleuth gave Orloff a short nod, then his eyes centered on Wallingford. "Your mention, when last we met, of the Deutsch Bank reaping rich dividends. The German banking house has call on four hundred thousand pounds' worth of gold in the vaults of the Bank of England. But the gold belongs to Hananish. From the treasure train, of course, and he's selling it twice, though this time with no consortium of banks and not with his partner Trelawney either. The Credit Lyonnais will get it from the Deutsch Bank. The Deutsch Bank gets it from the Bank of England, but the payment goes to Hananish. A major coup, but we've got him."

Wallingford grew pale and had trouble finding words. When they did come, it was not with the assured, businesslike manner that was his normal delivery.

"Mr. Holmes . . . I did not know about the three-way arrangement you outline; but it just won't work, you see."

His somewhat smug manner jarred, Holmes registered surprise.

"What won't work?"

"I see what you're driving at, sir. But Hananish can stop us cold. The four hundred thousand pounds in gold was deposited in his name in the Bank of England before the robbery."

There was dead silence in the room, and I confess

this startling statement actually caused me to hold my breath for a long moment. Holmes almost staggered back against the mantel, surprise a harsh and blatant thing on his expressive features. Good heavens, I thought. His whole case has been shattered by one unanticipated fact. The poor chap must be stunned.

Holmes's reaction was not what I anticipated. Instead, the palm of his right hand swept up to smite his forehead with a crack like a revolver shot.

"*Dumkopf*!" he shouted. When sore pressed, my friend resorted to exclamations in foreign languages.

A tinge of pink suffused the features of Wallingford, and the sleuth hastened to prevent a misunderstanding.

"Not you," he said, spearing the former confidence man with an outstretched finger. His digit swung in a half circle to tap his chest forcibly.

"Me!" Then his glowing eyes shifted in my direction and the shadow of a bitter smile creased his lips.

"If in future times, Watson, you choose to record this case history, you can write me down an ass."

If I had not known previously, this statement would have alerted me to how upset my friend was at himself. For he had used similar words when castigating himself for missing the mark on Colonel Walter in the matter of the Bruce-Partington plans.

Wallingford's face, a picture of consternation, was shifting from one to another of us, with a dazed expression, as though he had lost touch with reality. Orloff had a grim look of disbelief about him.

"You cannot mean that Hananish will elude our grasp," he said.

"Indeed no," replied Holmes quickly, and those

two words did much to rally my morale, momentarily very low.

Holmes's long stride took him to the desk, and he gazed at it as though beset with a number of necessary actions and choosing which one to seize on first.

"Now, finally, I have the right perspective regarding this case, and the errant threads that have nagged at me are unraveled."

There was a longish pause as Holmes communed with himself. Then his hawklike face rose and his eyes enveloped us.

"Orloff, you'd best be off to the Diogenes Club and relate our findings to my brother."

Holmes passed the letter he had received the night before to the security agent.

"Mycroft has developed an interest in the Deutsch Bank and could well find Wally's information of value. You might tell him that Watson and I have the matter of the stolen gold in hand."

"What can I do, sir?" asked Wallingford.

"Accompany Orloff. The Deutsch Bank has proved revealing to us. Possibly you can unearth some connection between the Germans and the financial manipulations of Trelawney and Hananish during the period the former was alive. My brother has certain connections, which you will find helpful."

A quick glance passed between Wallingford and Orloff, and the American responded dryly, "So I've learned."

The urgency in Holmes's manner was communicative, and both men rapidly vacated the premises.

Holmes was fiddling in his desk and suddenly turned to me.

"Now it is you and I, old friend, as it has been so many times before. Another journey is called for."

"Shall I throw some things in a valise?"

"Your Smith-Webley in a handy pocket will be enough."

There was the sound of rapid footfalls on the stairs, and Slim Gilligan appeared in the half-open door to our chambers. Now I understood Holmes's actions at the desk. He had some sort of alarm signal rigged up with the house next door.

"Slim," said my friend, "I've need of Burlington Bertie and Tiny."

"They were on the night shift, guv," responded the cracksman, taking the unlit cigarette from behind his ear. It occurred to me that I had never seen him light it.

"Contact them, good fellow, and have them take the first train available to Brent in Essex. I'll have them met at the station."

Gilligan had been with Holmes too long not to sense a crisis. "Anythin' fer me, guv?"

"Let's make sure this building isn't blown up, Slim. That Lightfoot rascal is still at large."

"Right, Mr. 'Olmes." Gilligan was gone.

So, I thought, it's back to the scene of the crime.

Holmes was spinning the dial on the safe and took a short-barreled revolver from its interior, placing it in the pocket of his tweed coat. His action prompted me to hasten upstairs to my sleeping quarters to remove my army-issue hand gun from the drawer in my bedstand. It was not often that Holmes went armed, but there was much about this strange case that departed from the norm.

Chapter 15

❧

The Lightning Colt

DURING OUR train trip to Essex, Holmes had been uncommunicative. I could not decide whether he was lost in thought regarding the robbery and subsequent events or whether, in keeping with his frequent practice, he had thrown his brain out of gear and switched his thoughts from the case on the theory that further cogitation would not be advantageous. When I had rejoined him in our sitting room prior to our departure, he was in the process of instructing Billy about a cablegram, and I deduced that it was to Dandy Jack, our only acquaintance in Brent. Such proved the case, since the aged four-wheeler and bay horse were at the station when we alighted, along with the familiar driver.

"Where to, gents?" he queried when we were seated in the conveyance.

"The end of the spur line."

"I figgers you mean by the tin mine," said the driver, gigging the bay into motion.

"When you've dropped us there, return to the station," said Holmes. "There will be two more men coming, and you are to bring them to the same place."

"Few folk come to Brent, but in case, how'll I know . . ."

"Oh, you'll spot them," I said, with an inward smile. "Just look for the widest man you've ever seen."

Dandy Jack merely nodded.

"Have there been strangers in the area of late?" inquired Holmes.

"None that I've seen." Holmes did not press the matter, and finally, our driver felt impelled to make a conversational contribution.

"I've nosed 'round, sir, and give the matter more thought. At tavern every night, there's palaver fer fair."

"About how the gold was removed from the boxcar." It seemed to me that Holmes made this statement with a certain satisfaction.

"Aye, sir. If I'm any judge, every man jack in these parts is as puzzled as I am."

Holmes nodded as though he had anticipated this. Silence fell, broken by the clip-clop of the sturdy bay and the intermittent calls of song birds.

When Dandy Jack deposited us at the clearing that marked the end of the spur line, he tipped his battered hat and went about his return trip in accordance with my friend's instructions. The clearing and its deserted buildings seemed as they had been on our last trip to this place. At that time, Holmes's attention had been much given to the end of track and the area where the boxcar had been discovered. Now he seemed interested in the stretch of ground between there and the small hill with the rock-filled entrance to the abandoned tin mine. But then, he had paid scant attention to it previously. I doubted if he expected to come up

with a clue at this late date, and felt that he shared
that thought.

"There is really little we can do until the boys get
here, Watson, though I did want to get to the spot
as soon as possible."

But it was not Bertie and Tiny who arrived.
Rather, it was another voice that called out and
succeeded in startling me no end, for I was convinced that we were alone in this deserted spot.

"Mr. Holmes. Dr. Watson," was the cry that
surprised me as we were making our way toward
the mine entrance.

From the woods on one side of the hill, Richard
Ledger appeared on the run. In one hand was the
Beals revolving rifle I had seen him use so effec-
tively.

Holmes and I came to a stop, and as Ledger
reached us, there was an added complication.

"Very slow, Ledger," said a strange voice. Clued
by the direction of the sound, my eyes flashed to the
top of the hill. Standing there was a tall and
swarthy man with an Enfield rifle pointed directly
at the three of us, as were the guns in the hands of
the two men standing beside him. There was no
sound for a long and nerve-racking moment, and
the whole scene became a frozen tableau. Then
Ledger, with a shrug that might have meant anything, reached out slowly with the hand carrying
the Beals rifle. He was facing Holmes and myself,
his left side toward the hill and the menacing men
atop it. Then he pitched the rifle some distance
from him. A moving object attracts the eye; and I
fancy the riflemen instinctively watched the falling
weapon, perhaps in anticipation that it might fire
when it hit the ground.

Ledger's left hand, resting on the lapel of the
unbuttoned top coat he was wearing, moved the

garment slightly away from his body and I saw a holster attached to his belt in front with the handle of a revolver pointing toward his right side. Simultaneous with this movement, his right hand flashed to the exposed gun butt, then reversed direction in a border draw. As the muzzle cleared the leather, it was already pointing in the direction of the hill. Of a sudden, there was a drumbeat of sound. Not single shots, but what seemed like a continuous roar. In a moment like this the eye transmits the image to the brain with a speed akin to that of light, which is a good thing since it all happened at once.

In but a fraction more than one second, five shots burst from Ledger's gun. The first shattered the rifle in the hands of the swarthy man. The second caught his right-hand companion in the forehead, passing out through the top of his head. The third one found the last of the trio in the vicinity of his left breast pocket. The fourth caught the swarthy man in his mouth and plowed into his brain, while the fifth blew its way between his eyes, making an obscene hole going in and a much larger one going out.

It was unbelievable, but there were three dead men on top of that hill before the first body hit the ground.

An unreal silence claimed the clearing and the hill on one side of it. There was the smell of cordite that wrinkled my nostrils. Then, from a silver beech on top of the hill, a bird trilled questioningly, as though to inquire what was going on. You'll never understand, little feathered friend, I thought. You'll also be quite surprised if you flit to the ground, for the green of the turf is being stained a darkish red.

Ledger blew on the muzzle of his gun and began

to slide it back into its holster when I found my voice.

"Pardon me," I said, in a higher tone than is customary for me. I gestured toward the revolver. "May I?"

As he handed me the weapon, from the corner of my eye I noted Holmes regarding me strangely.

"Double-action Colt Lightning," I said.

".41 caliber," replied the gunfighter. He was matter-of-fact about it, and his manner, after this moment of awesome violence, was unperturbed, like a workman who has performed a familiar task.

His eyes, said to be the gateway to the soul, reflected no flame of exhilaration or dancing sparks of triumph. Just twin pools, unruffled and unrevealing, though the color might have been an even lighter blue than I had noted previously. From a dim recess of my mind, two words stumbled forth. *Killer eyes.* Perhaps the title of some ha'-penny dreadful subconsciously noted on a bookstore stand. Perhaps words out of context from a description of a bird or beast of prey. I felt I understood them better now.

I indicated the butt of the gun questioningly.

"Parrot-beak handle," the man said. "I fancy it."

I swallowed. "Five shots in one and one-fifth seconds. I read somewhere that it had been done."*

Holmes was looking towards the hilltop.

"They've had it," said Ledger as I returned his gun to him.

"I can certainly believe that," replied Holmes.

The sleuth walked over and retrieved the rifle with which Ledger had distracted the three strangers. Silently, I commended him for this action. Though the immediate peril was removed, the

---

*Watson was right, for the time has been recorded, and with the same double-action model he was holding in his hand.

situation was still tense and I fingered the Smith-Webley in my pocket nervously.

Gesturing toward the hill, Holmes posed a question. "You didn't come with them, I take it?"

"After them. Your mention of that Michael fellow is what got me on their trail. The tall man was Jack Trask, who was on the Wellington Club team. Served in Egypt and later with the Legion in Africa. Surly chap with a shady background, but that's not unusual for a Legionnaire. The other two I don't know. Couldn't figure out why they came here either."

"That, I know," replied Holmes.

"Guess you know about me, too," said our rescuer.

As Holmes nodded I felt impelled to offer a remark, which drew another strange look from the sleuth.

"Not everything. It may not be necessary that we do. You are not Ledger, of course."

"He died in my arms. We were on the same side, you see, and we lost. I'd grown to know him well. He had no kin, and there were too many wishing for me to join Ledger, so I took his papers and got away."

"It was you who worked for the Kimberly people."

The man confirmed Holmes's statement with a nod. "They didn't know Ledger, and as soon as they put a gun in my hands, they accepted my identity without question."

An unrelated thought came to mind and forced its way to my lips. "Was your friend Ledger as good as you?"

There was a philosophical acceptance in his eyes along with a tinge of sadness. "Ledger's dead and I'm alive."

Holmes had strolled in the direction of the rock-clogged entrance to the abandoned mine. I surmised that the pseudo-soldier appreciated the absence of further questions regarding his, shall we say, colorful background. He now posed a question of his own.

"What were they doing here, Mr. Holmes?" He gestured toward the hilltop, and I winced at the thought of the three corpses growing cold in the afternoon sun.

"They were sent to remove evidence," replied the sleuth. "We'd best get started on the job at hand, for we can do some of it at least."

Holmes leaned the Beals rifle against a rock and began to remove his coat. I judged what he was about and started to do the same, as did our companion, but Holmes had another thought.

"Sir," he said, "and for want of another name, I must call you that; in a short time there will be others present. It might be expedient if you are not here."

The imposter could not supress an exclamation of surprise. "You're letting me go? What of the gold robbery?"

"You were no part of that," said Holmes. "Though it is my thought that you might put some distance between yourself and England."

Holmes overrode a half-formed interruption of mine.

"Not that I'll be after you, but it is possible that someone else knows of your masquerade. Had the robbery gone amiss, you would have made a splendid cat's-paw and might still serve as a red herring in the matter."

The gunfighter was nodding in agreement with Holmes's words, as was I.

"What about the bodies?" persisted the man.

This time he did not gesture toward the hill, which was throwing a first shadow on the three of us.

"The idea of a trade suggests itself," replied the detective, and despite the seriousness, nay grimness, of the moment, there was a flicker of humor about him. "That gun of yours Watson seems so familiar with. You might give it, with its spent cartridges, to my medical friend." His long fingers extracted the revolver he had in his ulster pocket; and Holmes extended it, butt first, to the marksman. "This may not suit your fancy, but it is loaded. I seldom carry firearms anyway."

Our youthful-looking companion seemed uncomfortable. "There's not many that hands me a loaded gun, Mr. Holmes."

"I'm sure you'd feel naked without one," said my friend in a brusque tone. Then his manner was relieved by a smile. "You understand that Watson, by virtue of this arrangement, will gain considerable notoriety not really his due."

Holmes's eyes swiveled toward me. "I picture you, good chap, as going down in history as the fastest gun on Baker Street."

"I say now, Holmes," was all I could come up with because of a wave of pride—not prompted by the ridiculous situation that Holmes was joshing about, but for my friend. He was not always the relentless man hunter that the journals pictured with such ghoulish glee.

The former employee of the B & N Railroad released the holstered gun, affixed with a clip to his belt, and passed it to me. Holmes looked at him for a long moment and then said, simply, "Goodbye."

The sleuth turned with an abrupt movement and began to push at one of the sizeable rocks blocking the entrance to the mine. I stepped closer to the

American, lowering my voice. Possibly Holmes did not hear me.

"Good-bye, McCarty."

For the first time since our paths had crossed, there was genuine humor on the man's face.

"I had a mind you knew." He clasped my outstretched hand, and I was surprised. He had spent his life in the outdoors and riding back trails at that, yet his palm and the inside of his fingers were as soft as a baby's or a safecracker's.

"Thank you, Doctor."

Retrieving the Beals rifle, he strode into the surrounding woods without a backward glance. His shoulders might have been slightly bent from the thought of the twisted trail behind him and the rocky road ahead. He can make it, I thought, if he but gets free. A legend does not die with ease.

Tossing my top coat on the ground, I joined Holmes in pushing and tugging at obstructing rocks.

Chapter 16

❧

All Fools Together

NOT LONG thereafter we heard the sound of Dandy Jack's four-wheeler. Holmes flicked perspiration from his brow, for we had made a fair start at the job. Retrieving his coat and donning it, he indicated for me to do the same. When the bay horse drew up in the clearing, there was no obvious indication as to what we had been about.

Dandy Jack's eyebrows were raised and he threw a patient glance heavenward, for the poor man obviously wondered if he was working for a circus. Burlington Bertie hopped from the carriage with a welcoming smile on his lips and a wise look in his eyes. He was a wedge of a man and brawny, but destined to be recorded in the eyes of an observer as nondescript in size, for with him was his younger brother. Tiny's broad face had a childlike serenity about it, with wide and innocent eyes and an anxious smile that seemed painted on. His smallish head topped a short but massive neck that disappeared into anthropoidal shoulders and a chest that could have modeled for a sculpture of Hercules. His short legs had to be like steel girders to support his bulk, and he removed himself from the carriage with dainty grace. Tiny was forced to maneuver with care, for if he unwittingly leaned against a tree, it might become uprooted. The bay horse threw a backward glance of relief when Tiny was supported by mother earth, and it whinnied and flicked its tail as though eager to depart.

The horse's wish was granted by Holmes, and his driver must have thought he was in charge of a shuttle service.

"It is back to Brent, Dandy Jack," said Holmes. "Locate that constable you mentioned."

"Sindelar," replied the worthy, as though life held no more surprises.

"Tell him a hearse is needed, but there is a doctor present who will sign the death certificates."

Dandy Jack's lethargic acceptance of all things was jostled by this, and he glanced around hastily in search of the bodies suggested by Holmes's words. He seemed relieved when he did not locate them.

"Tell Constable Sindelar that I will explain the matter to him. Best give him my card," Holmes added, passing one to the startled driver. "Since my party will be returning to London shortly, I will inform Scotland Yard, for they have an interest in what has transpired."

Thrusting the card into a patched pocket, Dandy Jack reined his steed around and departed with more alacrity than he had on his last return trip.

The sleuth now indicated the mine entrance to his two associates. "We have to get inside there," he stated, and that is all he had to say.

Tiny, with Burlington Bertie in his wake, moved toward the hill like an ocean liner, giving the impression that he might just walk through it. It occurred to me that I had never heard this goliath speak, though he certainly understood Holmes's words and had some private method of communication with his brother, who frequently interpreted his thoughts.

If Bertie did all the talking for the twosome, the former smash-and-grabber and wharfside brawler did not have to do much work. Tiny went at the mine entrance like a construction machine, and Holmes had to step lively to avoid flying rocks as he supervised the effort. I withdrew to a safe distance, for my energies, obviously, were not needed.

Holmes and I, without the boys from Limehouse, would have been unable to force our way into the mine; and I wondered how the bodies on the hilltop had intended to perform that task, for surely that had been their idea before our arrival. I also wondered why Holmes had been so sure that the gold in the vaults of the Bank of England had come from the treasure train, for now it was obvious, even to me, where his mind was leading him.

A cessation of activity within the mine prompted me to rejoin the threesome. The entrance was now clear enough, and ahead yawned the dark abyss of the main shaft.

"We've need of light on the scene," said Holmes.

Tiny turned, gently maneuvering his bulk around me, and disappeared through the entrance. He treated a statement from Holmes like an excerpt from the graven tablets of the divine commandments. His " 'Tis said, 'tis done," philosophy was certainly helpful in matters like the one we were involved in.

Within the dim mine interior I saw Holmes looking at Bertie questioningly and there was a flash of the man's teeth in response. In the distance, we all heard the rending protest of timber savagely being torn asunder. Then Tiny was at the mine entrance, his hair so blond as to be almost white. In his hand was the end of a limb, which I judged he had wrenched from a fallen and dead tree. Its butt was coated with a resinous jellylike substance.

"Good thought, lad," exclaimed Bertie. Quickly gathering some dead leaves that had blown into the mine, he crumpled them in his hand, igniting them with a sulfur match that he flicked against a stubby and dirty thumbnail.

Breathing on the small fire he had produced, Bertie thrust the limb into it and, in a moment the viscous sap burst into flame.

He passed the improvisation to Holmes. "Here it be, sir, fer you're the torchbearer 'round 'ere."

With Holmes in the lead, we cautiously worked our way into the mine, and I viewed the aged timber supports with some trepidation, I'll tell you. We did not have far to go. At the head of the side tunnel was a wagon, looking incongruous in this setting. Within, neatly stacked, were wooden boxes nailed shut. At a signal from Holmes, Tiny had one out of the wagon and on the floor of the tunnel. The sleuth held his torch high to illuminate the scene as the giant's eyes swiveled to the detective for further orders. Evidently, he received them in a glance, for one huge hand seized the top of the box, tearing the wooden cover off with a casual movement.

Within was metal, reflecting the torchlight, though it lacked the luster of the whitish-yellow substance I had seen when viewing the golden tablet during our Egyptian adventure.

"What's this, some hardware shipment?"

"Isn't it the gold?" I exclaimed.

"Naught but brass, Watson."

Blast the man, I thought with a surge of irritation. Whereas I was astonished, Holmes gave no evidence of any surprise at all.

"We've seen what we need to," he said. "Now I want this place sealed up again before Constable Sindelar and his people arrive."

As we hastened from the depths of the abandoned tin mine, Holmes passed a cautionary remark to us all.

"We've not even been within the mine, mind you. Nor are we interested in it. We have just been guarding three dead bodies until the authorities arrive."

We were outside now, and Bertie glanced at the sleuth questioningly. "I been wonderin' what the hearse be fer."

"Sober reminders of the prowess of the fastest gun in Baker Street."

I sighed in exasperation. Holmes picked strange moments for his clumsy witticisms, but he did seem to enjoy a private joke a bit more than most. Personally, I felt his reference to the corpses was black humor indeed.

Our departure for London was not inconvenienced in any way. The local constable was obviously awed by the presence of the master man hunter and accepted Holmes's version of the incident without question. He did state that he would forward a written report to Inspector Hopkins at the Yard, and I sensed that he was relieved to be able to place the matter in the hands of others.

We rode in the last car of the late afternoon train and were its only occupants, so no rural inhabitants were panic-stricken by the presence of Tiny. I did note that the conductor, having performed his official duties, shunned our car like a plague. Tiny promptly fell asleep, his head on his brother's shoulder. Considering the way he had thrown rock out of the mine and then back in it, some rest seemed justified. Out of deference to the slumbering giant, I did not plague Holmes with questions, which was a good thing since I do believe the sleuth seized the opportunity for forty winks himself.

Back in the comfortable and welcome confines of Baker Street it was another matter, for now I would not be denied. However, the number of my queries had been reduced, having thought on the matter to the best of my ability.

"Look here, Holmes," I said as I placed a whiskey and soda on the candle table by his chair. "I understand now that the gold shipment on the B & N was bogus . . ."

"Something I should have deduced from the start," said my friend, and there was a bitter tone to his voice.

"I'll not swallow that, for you are always chiding yourself for not immediately seeing through the most intricate schemes."

"If I do, I am wrong," was his surprising response. "To be misled by cunning is no crime. But when a misdeed involves a glaring error and I do not seize upon it, that is another matter."

Holmes's conviction did not dent my assurance this time.

"Hananish sent four hundred thousand pounds in gold to the Bank of England before the false shipment. Why that sum, by the way?"

"Because that's all there was. Hananish and Trelawney agreed to contribute one hundred thousand pounds to the consortium, which they never did because their reserve fund was elsewhere. The four hundred thousand was from the other banks of the combine."

"Neat, that. The conspirators had no financial involvement at all."

"Hananish told us there was no risk involved. I'll wager he had a silent chuckle in the telling."

"I take it the metal was delivered to Hananish by the west coast banks and sent from there to London."

"Correct. When the actual gold was safely tucked away in the Bank of England, Hananish sent the spurious boxes, suitably weighted, of course. Upon arrival in London, he had them transferred to the B & N Railroad and took out a policy for the listed worth of the shipment, five hundred thousand pounds, with Inter-Ocean. That's where he made his mistake."

"I fail to see it."

"Then, Watson, we were all fools together. Wasn't it suspicious that he didn't insure the shipment from Gloucester to London? There was just as much chance of a robbery during that trip as there was when the cargo went from London to Great Yarmouth."

I clasped my brow with my hands in anguish. "Of course."

"You are now mimicking my actions of this morning and thinking the same thoughts." This idea served to dispel Holmes's dark mood. "But come, the future is where our thoughts must lie."

"Half a mo'," I exclaimed. "The thieves took the crated brass from the boxcar and transferred it to the wagon. They maneuvered it into the mine and left it there."

"Blocking the entrance after doing so."

"What about the horses?"

"They turned them loose, stripped of their harness. You don't know your Essex farmer. Two unattended horses roaming about would go promptly into a barn. If someone came to claim them, there would be the oft-used-story of buying them from traveling gypsies."

I threw up my hands in capitulation. Holmes had all the answers.

After dinner that evening, it was Mrs. Hudson who announced the arrival of Claymore Frisbee, and I wondered if the sleuth had dispatched Billy on another mysterious errand.

The president of Inter-Ocean Trust was his urbane self when he entered our chambers and took a seat by the hearth fire, but there were lines of worry below the prominent cheekbones of his face. He was a good judge of moods, however; and Holmes's manner seemed to relax him. Perhaps the tot of quite superior brandy I secured for him helped. After all, he was our client.

"You suggested that I might toddle over 'round this time," Frisbee said after the exchange of customary pleasantries.

Holmes admitted to this. "Relative to the treasure train policy, you are . . . I believe the expression is 'off the hook.'"

Frisbee produced a heartfelt sigh of relief and allowed me to secure another brandy for him.

"That's welcome news, for it's a sizeable sum and would have put us under some strain, I'll admit. Who stole the gold?"

"Let me tell you," responded Holmes.

And he did in his precise manner, with no extraneous words or thoughts either. At several points during the recounting Frisbee was hard pressed to contain himself; and at the conclusion he did rather explode in amazement.

"You mean the B & N people and Scotland Yard have been running around looking every which way for the gold, and it was never on the train at all?"

"Comforting, wouldn't you say, since it is safely resting in the Bank of England."

"You're going to turn the matter over to Inspector Hopkins of the Yard?"

Holmes shook his head. "I haven't forgotten how they let Moriarty and Colonel Moran slip through their fingers, to say nothing of Lightfoot."

Frisbee registered puzzlement. "Lightfoot?"

"You wouldn't know him, and it's unimportant, though he may be mixed up in this. Only as a mercenary, however—a pawn."

"Albeit a dangerous one," I remonstrated.

Holmes waved this away. "There is some interest at Whitehall regarding this affair. I'm going to tackle Hananish tomorrow with the assistance of a special branch."

Holmes said *a special branch*. Frisbee thought he meant *the special branch*, just as my friend had intended him to.

"Well, if you're going to ring down the curtain yourself, I'm happy about it." Claymore Frisbee made to reach for his checkbook, but a gesture from the sleuth forestalled him.

"Let us settle accounts when we've written *finis* to this complex matter. There's a few jumps still to be taken."

"Regarding the insurance?" queried Frisbee with alarm.

"No, no!" You can pocket the premium and consider the matter at an end. But I've a wish to bring Hananish to heel. The grim reaper has dealt harshly with the ungodly, and there's a few left to testify for the Crown against him. In addition, I cannot stand in court and swear that the gold in the Bank of England came from the west coast banks, for I have no means of identifying the precious metal. However, I want to see Hananish show where it did come from, if not his fellow bankers."

"You've got him," stated Frisbee.

"I'll need your help." Holmes removed his gaze from the fire in front of him and regarded Frisbee keenly.

"You have but to ask," was the prompt answer.

"No news of the matter must leak out now. I wish to catch Hananish completely off guard, for it might unnerve him. In fact, let us spread a false trail. Let it be known that you are paying off the policy on the gold shipment. You could arrange an appointment for me to deliver the Inter-Ocean check to Alvidon Chasseur tomorrow, could you not?"

"What check?" sputtered Frisbee, again alarmed.

"There will not be one, but I have a little matter to settle with Mr. Chasseur. Relative to a disagreement between us as to who is the world's leading detective."

Frisbee, who had heard enough about the meeting between Holmes and the railroad tycoon to know what was going on, readily agreed to Holmes's request and made ready to depart, looking considerably more relaxed than when he had arrived.

Secretly, I groaned. Here we go again, I thought. Holmes accused me of having a pawkish humor, but he was not above a prank or two himself on occasion. I still shudder when I recall the hoax he perpetrated on Lord Cantlemere relative to the great yellow Crown diamond. The aged peer, who became one of Holmes's staunchest supporters, still contends that my friend's sense of humor was perverted.*

---

*Surely, in his later recording of this case, Watson became confused, for it is virtually certain that the Adventure of the Mazarin Stone took place after the turn of the century. It is obvious that this matter occurred somewhat before 1900.

I was helping Frisbee with his coat when Holmes posed a question.

"Have you had any dealings of late with the Deutsch Bank?"

Adjusting his muffler, Frisbee regarded the sleuth with surprise. "Strange you should ask that."

"How so?"

"They are solvent, all right. Their national economy is booming. Most of the pottery you buy now comes from German kilns, you know."

"Most of the waiters in our restaurants are German, for that matter," commented Holmes, for what reason I could not fathom.

"That so? One of the P.M.'s aides had a little talk with the banking commission recently about the size of German investments over here. They've been getting their fingers in a lot of things. Couple of steel firms in Birmingham were in need of financing but a while ago. The Deutsch Bank made overtures and the government had to step on the negotiations, diplomatically, of course."

Standing next to our visitor, my confusion must have been apparent. Holmes chided me for having a mirrorlike face as regards my inner feelings. Frisbee took pity on me.

"It's been a spell since we were allied with the Prussians and ever since Bismarck unified the German states, their empire has been gaining in strength. If Kaiser Wilhelm ever calls back the Iron Chancellor from Friedrichsruh and reinstates him, we could really be in trouble."*

Frisbee pondered for a moment on his words, then turned toward the door, only to turn around again toward Holmes.

*Proof that this case predates 1900, since Otto von Bismarck died in 1898—unless Watson got mixed up with dates, which he did tend to do on occasion.

"You know, we do have a number of Germans over here. A bit of a sticky thing if there's ever a war. Matter of intelligence, you know."

Holmes knew and so did I. As I let Claymore Frisbee out of our sitting room with a farewell, I thought of what he didn't know. Namely that Holmes's brother headed up the espionage department of the British government and was the second most powerful man in England. Holmes had never told me point-blank of his brother's real function; but ever since I had first met Mycroft Holmes in connection with that Greek interpreter matter in '88, I had realized that he did not just audit books in some of the government departments. I knew what special branch Holmes had in mind relative to Hananish in Gloucester.

Fatigue prompted me to sponge such thoughts from my mind. With the departure of our relieved client, I decided to retire for the night. The prospect of a return trip to Gloucester caused me to mouth a somewhat peevish complaint before doing so.

"Most of our time on this case has been spent in train travel, Holmes. It will be a relief to stay in London for a change."

My friend was staring into the fireplace, his mind I knew not where, but he responded.

"It all started with a train robbery, you know."

I could summon no retort to this and made my way to the upper story.

Chapter 17

❧

The Return to Fenley

THE BELLS of St. Mary-le-Bow were striking the hour when I suddenly sat upright in my bed. The room was pitch black and from the state of my bolster I knew that my sleep had been fretful. Something had been prodding at my subconscious, something I should tell Holmes. Then it came to me. The three men on the hill who had fallen before the American's flaming gun were unfamiliar to me. On that morning, not long ago, when I had been spirited away from the entrance to the Red Grouse Inn, I gained but a fleeting impression of the two men who had taken me so neatly and then, by intent, had left a broad trail behind them. But I knew they were not of the trio that had met their fate in Essex and were now being shipped to the morgue in London. This meant that Hananish had other bully boys at his beck and call.

The thought that had plagued me did not seem of importance when viewed with cold logic. Though my logic had acquired no fame, the room was cold—that I could state firmly. I knew that if I huddled under my blankets, sleep would prove the coquette indeed and but flirt with me through the remaining dark hours. Rather than waste my blandishments on the fickle mistress of the night, I searched with inquisitive toes for my slippers. Grateful for their fleece lining, I rose with a creak and a groan and trembled my way to the backless stool and my robe that rested on it. There was that silence that breathed at one, like a tangible thing rather than a total absence. A chill ran across the back of my shoulders, and I clutched my robe around me, stumbling in the darkness toward the door of my bedchamber. Down the back stairs I went with the thought that the dying embers of the hearth fire would be a welcome comfort. There was a dullish glow within the ashes of the back log that I stirred with the poker and then searched out the wood box for a length of birch. The bark of the soft wood was cooperative and soon there was a small but merry flame, which did little to offset the chill of the room but did raise my spirits slightly.

Throughout those untold generations before the wheel, the candle, the coming of the mechanical age, man had sought the healing balm of the unconscious when the sun departed from the western sky, sallying forth from caves when it reappeared in the East. Artificial light and a work cycle that could be altered to suit individual taste had turned night into day; but it was the memory of the genes, the schedule established through the evolutionary curve, that dropped one's metabolism to its lowest ebb during these eerie hours of early morning and prompted disjointed thoughts and errant wisps of vague memory as though from another life. A gleam caught my eye and I noted, in a sudden flaming of birch sap, the chambers and handle of the Colt gun shining at me from its leather holster on the bookshelf where I had placed it. For no reason I found myself composing a clumsy chanty and, more ridiculous yet, I sang it standing bent over the fire like a cackling Scrooge who had gone daft.

> Five shots near the mountain,
> They did the deed well.
> Five shots near the mountain,
> Three men went to hell.

Enough of this, I thought, crossing to the sideboard. The great silver urn felt warm to my hand and I poured a cup of coffee almost with anger. Here I was, by training a savior of life and, because of that meeting long ago, now embroiled in the danger and violence that was kith and kin to the profession of my most intimate friend.

In times past those twin footpads, blood and death, that tiptoed behind the world's only consulting detective had been shriveled in my mind's eye by the blinding light of my boundless admiration for Holmes's uncanny ability at observation and analysis, surely equal to the fabled tales of mythological necromancers. Now, had not the inroads of time, advance guard for the grim reaper my friend had mentioned to Frisbee, taken their toll? Fat and short-winded, could I now stand firm on the deck of that police boat roaring down the Thames in pursuit of the launch *Aurora*—firing my service revolver at that bestial native of the Andaman Islands and his master, the one-legged Jonathan Small? Could I now press the muzzle of a pistol to the head of one such as Patrick Cairns and force him to surrender? My self-doubts had me dizzy with recriminations, and the cup began to shake in my hand. Might I not be placing Holmes in danger?

That one moment when he depended on his companion of the years, might I not let him down?

But then, the memory of my old regiment came to me. You're spooked, Watson, I thought, and mouthing ineffable twaddle to yourself. Three men died today. More than three hundred spilled blood in the fatal battle of Maiwand, yours among it. More than three thousand went down in the second Afghan war. The cup stopped shaking, and I laced my coffee with a spot of Irish to mask its acrid taste.

It was then that I heard, in the complete silence, the downstairs door open. My first thought was Lightfoot, the late Moriarty's number one executioner. My second was my Smith-Webley upstairs. But then only Holmes and I, along with Mrs. Hudson, had keys to the street door; and the cunning dead-bolt lock had been set tonight, for I did it myself. But Holmes was asleep in his chamber, or was he? I had not seen him go to bed. Nonetheless, my eyes went to the Colt pistol that I had acquired under such strange circumstances on this day; but there was naught but spent cartridges in it.

I quickly ignited the lamp beside me, raising the wick, and then crossed to the fireplace to stand by the poker.

There was no sound on the seventeen steps leading upward to our first floor chambers, but the cat-footed Holmes wouldn't make any. I spoke out, and my voice had a slight tremor to it.

"Holmes?"

There was the sudden sound of key in lock and the door swept open to reveal my hawklike friend, who was chuckling.

"The lamplight put me on the alert, Watson, for I noted it under the crack of our door. I was standing without, pondering my next move, when I heard the welcome sound of your voice."

Suddenly his expression changed, and he regarded me anxiously. "Is something amiss, for this is an unusual hour for you."

"I could not sleep," I said, having no intention of telling Holmes of the defeatist tentacles that had menaced me with their debilitating embrace before I beat them back.

"Well then, since you're awake and I have not tried to sleep, let us be off."

I supressed a groan at this, determined to be as staunch a companion as I had ever been.

"Where were you, by the way?" I said, crossing toward the stairs.

"Anticipation, Watson, for I'll not be caught short again as I was but recently in this very room. Look for a possible alternative and provide against it. The first rule of criminal investigation."

I'd heard that before, and as before, it told me nothing. At the foot of the stairs leading to our bedchambers, I paused, then retraced my steps to take the holstered gun from the bookshelf. There were some boxer cartridges in my rolltop above that might be the right caliber.

We caught an almost deserted train out of Paddington that Holmes referred to as the "red-eye special," and I slept most of the way to Gloucester.

When we alighted at the Fenley station, dawn had not yet begun to stain the eastern horizon and there was a veritable symphony of the bird sounds that presaged its coming.

Standing on the dark station platform, immobile as a block of granite and quite as solid looking, was the figure of Wakefield Orloff. So, I thought, the security agent has preceded us. No wonder Holmes

seized the opportunity to leave early. Had he been
conferring with his brother, Mycroft, around the
witching hour?

Orloff greeted us and led the way through deserted streets of the village to the inn. There were
no other lights showing in Fenley, yet behind the
curtains in the Red Grouse I detected illumination.
A thought that I had previously dismissed came to
mind again and was reinforced when we entered
the establishment. The front room was not only
illuminated but populated as well. Five men, in
addition to the innkeeper and his wife, were in
evidence—sipping tea and munching sandwiches
made available by the lady. I had observed that the
inn was very well managed, but this was ridiculous. Unless my previous thought was well founded
and the place served as a headquarters for
Mycroft's people. It had to be such, for there was no
surprise at our arrival. The five men, strangers all,
shared a sameness that I recognized. Reasonably
young, they had a fit look about them and were
inconspicuously dressed. One would have had to
guess as to their business and been dissatisfied at
the conclusion arrived at. Surely their coats were
reversible, for I had seen Holmes use that trick.

I accepted a spot of tea. Holmes surveyed the
scene and nodded at Orloff, as though satisfied with
arrangements.

"How do we do it?" asked the security agent.

"We'll go now while it's still dark. You and your
men take the main house and stables. Let's not
have an alarm from some awakened groom."

"And you?"

"There is an annex to the main house where
wood work and such might be done if one had a
need for it. Watson and I will take a look there, then
join you."

One of the inconspicuous men, at a signal from Orloff, disappeared by the front door and I suspected our transportation was being arranged.

When we left the Red Grouse shortly afterward, two closed carriages were pulled up in front. Good heavens, I thought. Orloff has brought an army. But then we didn't know how many we were going against.

Orloff rode with Holmes and myself in the first carriage and the trip down the river road was not a longish one, as I had noted previously. When we all disembarked from the vehicles, I saw that Holmes had miscalculated slightly for there was a first light that revealed the substantial mansion we were interested in. Despite the predawn hour, there were lights and indications of activity within the building.

Orloff shot a glance at Holmes. "This tears it."

"Same plan," replied Holmes crisply. "It's important that no one slip away."

"A bit like that trap we sprung on Baker Street," observed the security agent. His men began to race to positions around the estate.

"And for rather the same reasons." Holmes motioned to me and we started up the drive, quickly moving to the close-cropped lawn to take advantage of the trees on the grounds. It was still sufficiently dark so that we could close in on the buildings without arousing the attention of anyone within. Close-by the main house, Holmes paused to take stock. There was no evidence of Orloff or his men, and I pictured them encircling the place and then closing in. What they intended to do with any gardeners or servants they came across, I could not imagine.

I indicated the lights within. "What has them stirring so early?" I asked.

"Three men went to Essex yesterday and there's no word from them. It may have shaken Hananish's confidence a bit. It's well that we are here when we are."

The sleuth indicated the annex he had mentioned, and I followed as he moved in a half trot from the front of the mansion to the side. The area that had caught his retentive eye was but one story, abutting the main building. Close on, I could hear some movement within; but there were no windows, so we moved to the end of the building and around it. There was one window there, which proved unrevealing. The dark interior we made out proved to be a small storeroom with lumber stacked in it, along with gardening tools. The side away from the driveway and well-tended grounds was the building's actual front. Now we saw light from a window and crouched beside it, carefully peering in. Over Holmes's shoulder I spotted one man seated under a wheel chandelier, its four lights providing bright illumination for the table he was working at. It looked like he was dismantling some sort of scales arrangement. There were saws and carpentry tools aplenty, and the place had a well-swept look.

Satisfied, Holmes drew back and then hunched over, almost on hands and knees, to pass below the window frame toward the door in evidence beyond. With some difficulty, I patterned my movements after his. By the door, however, I advanced a thought with gestures. Extracting my Smith-Webley from my coat pocket, I transferred it to my left hand. The door was not a heavy one, and I judged it was not locked. Moving to its other side, I indicated to Holmes that I could smash it open with ease and we could enter together. He indicated that this plan was as good as any. As I stepped forward with purpose, it occurred to me that the sleuth was not armed and our unified front served no purpose; but the plan was in action now and was, I recalled, favored by better constables everywhere. My heel smashed at the door, which sprang open under the impact; and I was in the room with my gun pointed at the man at the workbench. Holmes was at my right side. The man under my sights was completely surprised; and I was congratulating myself on a workmanlike job when my left hand, with the extended and menacing revolver, caught a terrible whack from a stout piece of wood in the hands of a pasty-looking fellow who had been in the vicinity of the door. The Smith-Webley dropped from my grasp, and my assailant kicked it toward the table, shielding his companion.

"Blimey," he said, "we's got visitors an' such an' early hour."

I recognized the voice, for it was the man who had dragged me into the carriage outside the Red Grouse.

His companion had whipped out a long-barreled hand gun, with which he was covering Holmes. I was bent over, my left wrist pressed to my side in anguish, but my blood was boiling. Almost without thought, my right hand passed under my coat to the holster affixed to my belt; and then the Colt gun was in my hand. As I started to rise from my crouch, I began to press on the trigger gently in preparation for a shot, but, dear heaven, the weapon took charge. It had been altered by some master gunsmith, and its action was as sensitive and skittish as a village maiden receiving her first kiss. It roared before I had a mind to fire, and continued to do so. The first shot smashed the revolver from the man's hand, and as I staggered back, the second shot separated the chandelier from the ceiling and it dropped, smashing him with frightening force. My pasty-faced friend made a lunge for the Smith-Webley on the floor only to have it jump from his grasp, and there was the eerie whine of a ricochet. My fourth shot blew the heel off his shoe.

I finally gained control over the weapon and terminated this needless firing, which the pasty-faced man found hard to believe. He was moaning, his hands pressed tightly over both eyes.

"My God, guv, no more. Mother in heaven, I gives up!"

His compatriot had already done so, and the upper part of his body was stretched out on the workbench, pinned down by the chandelier that had rendered him unconscious.

Suddenly the comforting presence of Wakefield Orloff was on the scene.

"I just circled the house, and I saw it through the open door. Where did you ever learn to shoot like that, Doctor?"

"Watson is a man of many talents," said Holmes. "The gunfire has stirred things up, of course."

Orloff reassured him. "No fear. We've bagged the servants. The ground floor is secured. As for the master of the house, I assume he is on the first story."

"Then we'd best confront him," said Holmes, "before Watson reloads and decides to recreate the famous battle of the O.K. Corral."

I gave Holmes a disapproving look as I scooped up my bullet-nicked Smith-Webley. Orloff dragged the pasty-faced man, still pleading for his life, from the floor and marched with us toward the lair of Burton Hananish, west coast banker, among other things.

Chapter 18

❧

The Roar of Sound

THE MAIN hall of the Elizabethan mansion was a scene of quiet disorder. The butler, who had greeted us on our previous visit, was seated, as were two housemaids. This breach of decorum was explained by the watchful presence of one of Orloff's men. The servants shared a stolid resignation. Orloff had words with his assistant, no doubt relative to the disposition of the pasty-faced captive he had in tow. Holmes and I made for the grand staircase and the first floor.

In an upstairs drawing room that evidentally served as an office, we found Hananish going through the drawers of a varqeano chest, which had been altered to serve as a desk. I judged the piece to be of the time of Phillip the Second, for there was the San Juan Campostella shell design in the pulls and intricate carvings made by use of gold leaf. Moorish cabinetmakers were famous for their excellent seventeenth-century work and for their tendency to incorporate secret drawers, a practice well known to Holmes.

The banker was not unattended, for standing

behind his wheelchair was a rather loutish-looking
fellow, powerful enough to have served as a boun-
cer at Sydney Sid's beer and gin hall in Limehouse.
Hananish attempted to preserve his saintly facade
when we burst in upon him, but it was a struggle,
for the ends of his mouth were seized by an
uncontrollable twitch.

"Mr. Holmes, though chained to this chair, it is
obvious that my home has been invaded by a
veritable army. This is contrary to every . . ."

His voice dwindled out, for Holmes had waved
away his protestations with a gesture indicating
that they were but verbal fluff. The sleuth seated
himself in a Renaissance leather chair, also Spanish I judged, and proceeded to cut to the bone and
then the marrow of the matter.

"We waste time," he stated, and there was that
grim note of finality in his voice that I knew well.
"Not only ours, but the Crown's."

He indicated the mass of papers on the mitred
drop door over which Hananish's beautiful fingers
were fluttering as though to wish them away.

"We shall not tamper with those papers, please,
for now they are the property of the English court."

"This invasion of privacy . . ."

It was as though the man had not spoken, for
Holmes continued in his flat, factual manner,
which defied both interruption and contention.

"My eye has not played me false, and in that area
you find usable for carpentry are scales, remains of
packing cases—sufficient evidence to support the
chain of events I have linked together, so let us not
bandy about the word *circumstantial*. The dirty
tricks brigade you dispatched to Essex are no more.
The mine has been opened and the spurious gold
shipment revealed. It was an involved scheme,

which added to the risk, but you played for high
stakes.* It's all over, you know."

The man's parchmentlike complexion was tinged
by a sickly yellow cast, like something disinterred.
His eyes flicked to a portion of the disarray in front
of him, an instinctive and revealing movement that
I knew Holmes had not missed.

"The gold came to you for trans-shipment to
London from the west coast banks. You had the
ingots removed from the packing cases, which you
filled with brass, plus some lead I judge, to conform
with the weight of the gold. The precious metal was
recrated and sent to the Bank of England, with the
false shipment made at a later date. You had
already arranged the insurance with Inter-Ocean.
The wooden cases, with authentic freight markings
from their points of origin, were placed aboard the
B & N flyer, and there was no cause for alarm. All
seemed as it should be. If the shipment reached the
Credit Lyonnais, you would have been exposed. So
it was hijacked. A pretty plan. Once the hirelings
separated the boxcar from the treasure train, they
had no great problem as to the disposal of the loot,
for they merely dumped it in the abandoned mine
and took to their heels. The wagon and its worthless cargo might have rotted there for centuries had
I not taken on the case."

"But you did, Mr. Holmes." There was a flicker in
what had been lackluster eyes. This surprised me.
Holmes might well have been cast in the role of the
Archangel Gabriel at Jericho, for the banker's walls
were tumbling down.

"I said it was a pretty plan. The west coast banks

---

*High stakes? Four hundred thousand pounds alone converts into two
million dollars, and this before the turn of the century and the degenera-
tion of both currencies. Holmes may have been guilty of understatement
here.

would be paid. The Credit Lyonnais would receive the insurance, and the French, persistent when faced with a loss, would have been satisfied and merely looked elsewhere for their needs. Only to find you waiting for them with the gold they wished. It was a circuitous arrangement, with sales percentages at each way stop, but it finally led to you."

"You know of that?" There was another flicker in the tired eyes of that statuesque face, and a sardonic twist came to Hananish's cruel lips.

"I know everything." From Holmes's tone, I deduced that he believed his statement. A suspicion was forming in my mind that Hananish did not.

The sleuth had been leaning forward, and suddenly he was on his feet, his long arm snaking out to pluck a cable from under the banker's nervous hands.

"Ah-hah." There was satisfaction in his manner as his eyes flashed over the message then stabbed at the banker for a moment before returning to the words, which he read aloud.

"'The meddler knows all. Get out.'" Holmes dropped the cable on the desk surface and resumed his seat. "That warning came late."

"I am ill-suited to flight in any case," replied Hananish.

The flicker in his eyes had grown to a flare, and there was a look about him that raised the short hairs on the back of my neck. Then a shadow was cast by the morning sun through the door behind us. I knew Orloff was present and felt the better for it. An apparently unrelated thought sprang to mind. Holmes had discussed the Ripper matter, making it plain that his forte, reason and logic, was of scant use in tracking down one who was guided by neither. According to the rules of the game,

Hananish had had it and could now only hope for aid from an astute solicitor and eloquent barrister. But there was about his patrician features a look that alerted one with medical training. He had set himself up as a rural despot and, with his mobility taken from him, had dreamed great dreams like Timur the Lame. With a treasure like Monte Cristo's at his fingertips, he might well have pictured himself as the second coming of Moriarty. Now, as with the professor, Sherlock Holmes was shoving him from the chessboard as he reached for the king piece.

My throat suddenly dry, I tried to utter a warning, but events were too fast for me.

"Hilger," called Hananish in a frantic manner, yet a wave of seeming exultation washed his face.

The brute attending him moved toward me, for I was standing with an eye on the man. Then the shadow behind me became a shape in front of me and the deceptively squat figure of Orloff was in action. The servant reached a hand for him, which was his second mistake. His first was in moving at all. Suddenly the fingers of Orloff closed on the man's wrist and there was a twist that spun Hilger around, his arm bent behind his back. The security agent's right boot swept the man's feet from the floor and Hilger fell, his jaw crashing against the converted varqeano chest in the process. Orloff stepped back, allowing the body to slump to the floor. I noted a trickle of blood from Hilger's mouth and suspected a fracture at least. It had been nothing for Orloff, a mere warm-up; but he was not allowed to continue his act, which he performed with the polished ease of a variety entertainer.

Under cover of the scuffle, Hananish had reached for the chest and a panel had sprung open in it. Now he was armed, for in his hands was a twelve-bore double-barreled shotgun, with half of its twin cylinders sawed off. It was pointing right at Holmes, both hammers at full cock. What panicked me more than anything else was the conviction that Hananish intended to fire come what may. If he did, seventy-six grams of shot at point-blank range would tear Holmes to ribbons.

Both Orloff and I were frozen. Holmes, immobilized by his seated position, was impotent to act. Then, as though it were all a slow-motion pantomime, I saw the fingers of the banker tighten and the hammers fell. There was a roar of sound.

Chapter 19

❧

To the Lion's Den

THERE WAS more smoke than there should have been, and when it cleared, I saw why. The shotgun, a twisted and broken thing now, had burst and the full force of the powder and shot had exploded in Hananish's face. What was left would have made a shocking illustration for Washington Irving's *Legend of Sleepy Hollow*. Contrary to intent, it was Holmes who was Ichabod Crane, whilst Hananish was the headless horseman.

"Thank God," I choked.

Holmes mopped his brow with Irish linen, his hands steady.

"I was not meant to die," he said.

Holmes regarded what was left of Hananish for a brief moment and his chiseled features, so often willed into immobility, could not reject an expression of horror. I turned away, not only from the corpse but my companions as well, for I was overcome with emotion. What was mirrored in those fathomless green eyes of Orloff, I knew not. But I could imagine. He walked a lonely path, did Wakefield, and what friends he had stood now with him in this room of death. In his nerveless, often heartless mind I knew he echoed the words that I kept repeating fervently to myself.

"Holmes lives."

He did indeed and was now his old self, rallying us back to those duties that our destiny had ordained for us.

"We've got to keep a lock on this thing till we return to London."

Orloff indicated it could be done.

"Will you be returning with us?" asked Holmes.

"My men can handle this, and they know what to look for." As if in answer to the thought that came to my mind, he added, "Hananish is gone, but we've still got to tie up the bundle if only for the record." Orloff must have been considering the orders he was going to give, for he added almost inaudibly: "Your brother wishes me to remain by your side." A faint cloud passed over his face, and I knew he was berating himself. If not asked, he never advanced information, especially about his employer, the mysterious Mycroft Holmes.

In the carriage returning to Fenley and on the train back to London his remark gave me thought. The gold had been found, and those who stole it had come to an abrupt end. What now remained but the clearing up of details and the necessary tendering of information to the authorities involved? But, no, there was still Lightfoot McTigue at large.

I was leaning against the cushioned back of our compartment as I pondered on this. Orloff sat beside the door, his small, dancer feet flat on the floor and his body upright but completely relaxed. The bowler hat with its concealed steel rim, which was such a deadly weapon in his hands, was tilted over his eyes. The even cadence of his soundless breathing, revealed by the movement of his chest, convinced me that he was asleep. Holmes, legs outstretched, was by my side.

"I wonder where Lightfoot is at this moment?" he said softly as though reading my thoughts.

"Probably plotting your demise," was my automatic retort.

"The man has no bank for his emotions and only works for pay. When we clear up the treasure train matter, who's to foot his bill?"

I sensed that he was turning this thought over in his mind, and there was a considerable silence before he spoke again.

"We're one up on Lightfoot, you know, for he cannot realize that we are aware of his redheaded guise."

I tilted my head to survey him. My friend's eyes were closed.

"The Trelawney matter, and Michael's death as well, bore his trademark. He was hired to do both jobs and planned them well in advance."

"What leads you to that conclusion?" I muttered, out of deference to our sleeping companion.

"Ezariah Trelawney's stepson was first in line as a suspect when the banker's body was found. Right after him were Staley and Ledbetter, Trelawney's hereditary enemies. Michael had incurred the wrath of the artist Folks. But Trelawney was killed first and Lightfoot was on the scene in the redheaded disguise, which was created especially for the Michael killing. Ostensibly, the Trelawney case is closed. The Michael matter is up in the air; and Lightfoot must feel that the artist Folks is the prime suspect."

Now I followed Holmes's drift. McTigue, stylistically, performed his antisocial duties so that others got the blame. At this point he had no reason to think his presence was known.

The subject was of interest, spiced with an undercurrent of danger, but I chose this moment to fall asleep.

Back in our familiar surroundings, with a change of clothes and a suitable meal, I felt more ready to cope with whatever crossed our horizon. Holmes had departed for points unknown but returned to sit over coffee with me. Rather impatiently, I thought, though we had some time before leaving for our appointment at the Birmingham and Northern. With our harrowing adventure in Fenley now a part of the past, I summoned my courage. It was a personal question I had in mind, hence, delivered in a tentative manner.

"I've given more than a little thought to that near-fatal moment this morning, Holmes. Hananish's shotgun was an aged model. Do you feel his reducing the barrel length caused it to backfire on him?"

"Gratitude is what I feel."

Finally I got 'round Robin Hood's barn. "But there you were, looking down those twin barrels. What passed through your mind?" I was embarrassed when I said it, but who has not wondered what thought occurs when one stares at death?

Holmes took his time answering, and I was grateful for his treating my question seriously and not evading it with a light remark.

"I believe my first thought was that this was it, something that we all must come to eventually. *Debitum naturae.* Then I wished that it had not happened so soon. In that split second, I must have derived some satisfaction from the knowledge that I would be revenged with you and Orloff present."

"But you did think it was going to happen?"

Holmes indicated this was so, and I dropped the matter. His statement after Hananish had blown himself into eternity had been: "I was not meant to die." This was at variance with his words now and rather smacked of the fatalism of Eastern religions.

At this point, Billy announced Alec MacDonald, and my thoughts shifted to other matters.

"I'll take but a moment of your time, gentlemen," stated the Scot, and he meant it, for he did not remove his coat or cast a glance at the tantalus on the sideboard.

"News of Lightfoot?" inquired Holmes.

"Aye. I'm not happy dealing with informers, but there's times when it's the best we can do. There's this sister of a woman of McTigue's, you see. The whisper is that he's planning on crossing the Channel this very day. There's an alert out on him, but I'm not feeling hopeful in my bones."

"Nor I," said Holmes. "If he's making his getaway, he'll change his appearance, something Lightfoot is adept at doing."

"You think, then, the information is correct?"

"I choose to. His job is done; and he's been paid, you can depend on that. What more natural than his making for the Continent, where he's been safe for some years."

"We'll never grab him then."

"Not unless it is in transit. I'll buy the whisper, Mr. Mac, and release the watchdogs I've had around here for that reason."

MacDonald made to leave, but he had an exit line.

"I've had some boys in the neighborhood myself of late."

He noted Holmes's surprised reaction with satisfaction. "From time to time I have words with a certain master locksmith, you know." He was chortling as his heavy tred sounded on the stairs.

"Watson," said Holmes, "my friends conspire against me." He was not serious, of course, and proved it. "I do think MacDonald's constables were a trifle obvious standing in the entrance of Spears and Henry down the street. They really should have varied their station."

Now it was I who registered surprise and it was genuine.

"You noticed, then?"

"When I stop noticing, we're in trouble, good chap."

A tap on the door and another appearance of Billy prevented me from replying to this. I had no rejoinder in any case.

Our page boy handed Holmes a cablegram, which he opened eagerly. After a long moment of concentration, he folded the message and placed it in his pocket with satisfaction.

"Billy, fetch us a hansom. Dr. Watson and I are off to the lion's den."

"Mr. Orloff is waiting outside with one now, Mr. 'Olmes."

"I might have known," chuckled the sleuth as he waved me toward the door.

Chapter 20

❧

Denouement

THE COUNCIL room of the B & N Railroad was much as I remembered it; but then, despite all that had happened, our previous visit had been but eight days ago. The board of directors were not in evidence and that caught me up short. I figured Alvidon Chasseur for an exhibitionist and thought he might relish an audience when he received the Inter-Ocean payment and had the opportunity to laugh at Sherlock Holmes. Claymore Frisbee had set up our meeting for the ostensible purpose of paying the insurance claim. With the rail tycoon was a sallow-faced man that I earmarked with the title secretary. Also present was the grizzled old board member Chasseur had been conferring with on our first visit. This time the magnate rose to indicate our seats alongside the great oak table. As before, he ignored me completely but did direct a quizzical glance at Orloff.

"An associate," said Holmes, which seemed to satisfy Chasseur. Orloff did not sit at the conference table with us, but seemed much interested in a chest against the wall opposite the fireplace, obviously decorative, for it served no purpose. It was a fine old piece, of lowlands origin I thought, and surely with its original lock and key. I made note to check it for the name of the cabinetmaker, since they signed things in those days.

Chasseur decided to ignore Orloff as well, centering his large eyes on Holmes. There was a malicious twist to his thin lips.

"Our second meeting is under different circumstances indeed, Mr. Holmes. I will be frank. It is not quite the tidy wind-up one associates with he who is reputed to be the greatest man hunter of them all. By his own admission, I might add."

"We all make mistakes," replied Holmes, and I never expected to hear him say that. But then he was letting the pompous railroad man take in more wind before he punctured his balloon. "During my last visit, I labeled Colonel Moran as the finest shot our eastern empire had produced. At that time I had not seen your man Ledger in action."

"I would talk to you about that," said Chasseur excitedly. "Ledger has disappeared, and my railroad detectives are searching for him. Scotland Yard as well, for he has to be involved in the robbery."

"Before it was over he was, perhaps not in the manner you think."

Chasseur gave Holmes a strange look but decided not to pursue this. "Now to business, for my schedule is tight. The matter of the payment from Inter-Ocean."

"I don't have it," replied Holmes blandly.

"But Frisbee promised to . . ."

"He promised to honor your claim at this time if the gold was not found."

"That goes without saying."

"But I've found it, you see."

Chasseur leaned back in his chair and exhaled, and I'm blessed if it didn't sound like air escaping from a balloon. There was consternation on his face. I couldn't figure if he was amazed at recovering the shipment or disappointed at not being able to rub Holmes's nose in the ground.

"This cannot be one of those practical jokes I'm told you indulge in," he finally stammered.

"Hardly. It is a reasonably simple story. Most cases are, once solved. The participants may be familiar to you. Ezariah Trelawney, Burton Hananish, and Ramsey Michael were involved in a scheme to pirate four hundred thousand pounds' worth of gold from the west coast banks. There was another hundred thousand to be picked up from the Inter-Ocean insurance as well."

"But where is the gold, Mr. Holmes?"

"In the Bank of England."

"Wait, now! I did know Trelawney and Hananish, and the latter's deposit in the Bank of England is old news. But it was made prior to the B & N shipment."

"Your shipment was of crates of baser metal with little value indeed."

Now Chasseur's shrewdness became evident, for he grasped the situation immediately. "Amazing. This Michael you mentioned. He was murdered, for I read it in the papers. Trelawney was killed as well, a while back. Was there a disagreement between the conspirators?"

Chasseur thought on this for a moment, then pounded the table in front of him. "Divine intervention, that's all you can call it with Hananish dead as well."

"How did you know that?" asked Sherlock Holmes.

"Why, the news came to me at midmorning, I believe . . ."

"A cable, Mr. Chasseur," said the shallow-faced secretary.

"Exactly. If the three conspirators have met their end, you can understand my immediate thought regarding a higher power. But come, yours is the practical approach, and there must be a rational explanation. Trelawney was involved in the gold shipment, as was Hananish. What alerted you to this Michael fellow?"

"Something relative to his murder," replied Holmes.

"And you were able to tie the three together? The tales of your amazing professional powers are not overstated, sir. How did you do it?"

"They served in the same regiment in the Crimea. Also, their names were a clue. Relative to the Bible, you see."

"The Bible?" Chasseur appeared befuddled.

"You may recall that Nebuchadnezzar had brought to his court in Babylon certain of the children of Israel."

"Wait, Mr. Holmes, for I know my Bible well. You speak of Shadrach, Meshach, and Abednego. Good heavens, I see it! In Judah they were Hananiah, Mishael, and Azariah. That's what tied them together in your mind? Brilliant."

Holmes gestured in a modest manner, a cloak ill-fitting to his shoulders.

"It was a coincidence that would be hard to overlook. Like three ladies on a committee named Faith, Hope, and Charity. They would become known to each other, I'm sure."

Chasseur was regarding my friend, reluctantly I thought, with some awe. "With this thin thread you

tied them into the plot to swindle the Inter-Ocean,"
he said.

"Not exactly. Recall that there was someone else
associated with the three wise men."

The tycoon preened himself. "I do, sir. Let me
quote to you: 'And these three men, Shadrach,
Meshach, and Abednego, fell down bound into the
midst of the burning fiery furnace.

"'Then Nebuchadnezzar the king was astonished, and rose up in haste, and spake, and said
unto his counsellors, Did not we cast three men
bound into the midst of the fire? They answered
and said unto the king, True, O king.

"'He answered and said, Lo, I see four men loose,
walking in the midst of the fire, and they have no
hurt; and the form of the fourth is like the Son of
God.'"

Chasseur was regarding Holmes rather taunting-
ly. "Surely, sir, you are not suggesting that the Son
of God was in cahoots with three modern-day
bandits?"

"A scholarly rendition from the book of Daniel,
Mr. Alvidon Daniel Chasseur. My compliments."

I slid my hand into my coat pocket, gripping the
Smith-Webley, for now it was obvious. The impli-
cation was not missed by the rail magnate; and I
thought he paled slightly, though he retained his
hauteur. Holmes did not wait for a response.

"It was Daniel, renamed Belteshazzar, who came
to Babylon with the others; and it is the fourth man
I'm after. He has to exist, else nothing makes sense.
Ezariah Trelawney was a miserly soul who never
left his native village of Shaw. Hananish was a
cripple, entrenched in Fenley. Michael was very
much of the London scene. Unless they transacted
their considerable business by post, there had to be
a connective link. Also, the well-planned robbery

depended on a knowledge of the time and route of the treasure train, plus the plan to guard it evolved by Ledger."

"Trelawney was a stockholder in Birmingham and Northern. So was Hananish," sputtered Chasseur; but his argument sounded weak, even to him.

"Probably Michael as well," replied Holmes. "Which brings us to the nub of the matter. There are too many stockholders of the B & N. You were originally financed by a cadre of speculators in Scotland. The Scotch are of the opinion that they hold seventy-five percent of your rail empire. But how about the financial group in Cornwall? You attended a stockholders' meeting there recently; and I learned they hold around eighty percent of the outstanding stock of the B & N, or think they do. Your three partners have large blocks of the company as well."

Chasseur's face was becoming a fiery red. "Mr. Holmes, for a presumably clever man you are indicating a naïveté about financial matters. Books are inspected. What kind of sleight of hand do you fancy I indulged in?"

"Your words are apt," responded the sleuth. "The B & N was constantly expanding, engulfing other rail concerns. As long as you were altering your corporate structure, a clear picture could not be obtained, for you obfuscated matters with preferred issues, convertibles, deferred bonds, and all the prestidigation of which you are an obvious master. It had a disadvantage in that the moment you ceased to expand, someone would be able to figure out that your original stock issue did not incorporate one hundred percent of the company, but two or three times that amount. That is why, right now, you are involved in the acquisition of the London, Tilbury and Southend Railroad."

"How did you learn of that?" spat Chasseur, with a venomous look at his secretary and then the speechless member of the board sitting beside him. Both, for some time now, had looked like they wished they were somewhere else. Somewhere far away.

"Ledger mentioned the L, T & S," said Holmes, "and I checked them out. The offer you made that concern was tempting indeed, but involved a relatively modest initial outlay, with the bulk to come in time payments. That's what you were buying— time. The London, Tilbury and Southend, as a matter of procedure, had one of their officers run a check on your assets. A pleasant man, I had quite a talk with him. He was much impressed by the four hundred thousand pounds in gold in the Bank of London, deposited to the account of Burton Hananish but with a deed of transfer to the B & N Railroad. Then there was more than that in promissory notes from the Credit Lyonnais. He gave an A-1 report to his superiors because, just at the time of his survey, you had all that collateral available, courtesy of your partners, Hananish and Trelawney. With the L, T & S in your grasp, you are ready to do business with the Deutsch Bank."

The first vestige of panic was forcing its way past Chasseur's guard and into his eyes.

"German banks are attempting to secure a foothold in British industry and transportation ranks high in their plans. The Deutsch Bank has agreed."

Since Chasseur just regarded him dumbly, Holmes extracted the cable he had received prior to our departure from Baker Street.

"You may not even know as yet, so let me inform you of the news obtained by an operative of mine in Berlin at this moment." He read the cable.

"'Cincinnati committed projection ten biggest credit mark BN.' Signed, Wally."

Chasseur had recovered some of his composure; but there was a grim look about him, as though all exits were being blocked.

"You can't siphon any sense from that gibberish," he said with a sneer.

"I can because it is the simple odd word code, which my associate knew I would recognize. The odd words in the message relate to the true words intended. The even words are legitimate. My correspondent is American, by the way, which aided my decoding. The first word, *Cincinnati*, is bogus, but in America that metropolis has a considerable German population, so I substituted *Germans*. *Projection* gave me a moment's thought till I came up with *extension*. I expected a message relative to a sum, and the biggest number that comes to mind is million. So we have: Germans committed extension ten million credit. *Mark* must mean *line*, and the BN refers to Birmingham and Northern. With a ten million credit line from the Deutsch Bank plus the London, Tilbury and Southend acquisition, you could have muddled your books for years and kept your unsuspecting stockholders at bay as well."

Chesseur was breathing heavily, like a bulldog with asthma.

Holmes lit a cigarette in an airy fashion.

"You might have gotten away with it, you know. Your hired assassin, Lightfoot McTigue, disposed of Trelawney and Michael, since you didn't need them anymore. This morning he took care of Hananish as well."

"But the banker shot at you, Holmes," I exclaimed involuntarily.

"I was not meant to die, Watson. Lightfoot had blocked the barrels of the shotgun, probably with lead, though wooden plugs would have done the job. There was a cable from Mr. Chasseur, here, warning Hananish of my coming. The man was teetering on the brink mentally, you see."

Holmes's somber eyes returned to Chasseur.

"You knew the cable would panic him and that he would use his hidden weapon. How simple to have him do away with himself. You must have felt relieved when McTigue cabled you that Hananish was dead and, his job done, that he was leaving for the Continent."

Chasseur's blazing eyes fixed his secretary with a fierce glare. "You talked, you fool."

"Mr. Chasseur, I've never even met Mr. Holmes."

"Don't blame others, Chasseur. It was just a matter of pulling all the pieces together. Hananish's books are being gone over. Trelawney's have already been closely inspected by a man who can smell a swindle from a distance. This interview has been a lengthy one, but for a purpose. As we talk, officials are sequestering your records and files by virtue of a special warrant issued from Whitehall. The Crown considers England's transportation system vital to national security. I cautioned them to locate your payment to McTigue, which must have been made today. I'm rather interested in how much you gave him for killing three men."

Chasseur's face had reflected a kaleidoscope of emotions but was now almost placid, resigned.

"I suppose, in the fashion of Dr. Watson's published case histories, that you were on to me from the very start?"

"I should have been," admitted Holmes. "Why did you, reputed to be astute, go to such pains to alienate me from the case? For that is what you did at the very beginning."

Chasseur shrugged and reached casually toward

a small drawer on his right, but I was having none of that. My Smith-Webley came into view with rather good speed, I thought. Somehow my alertness did not seem to phase the man, for he smiled a crooked smile and displayed a rubber casing in his left hand. It had a button arrangement on the top over which his thumb hovered. I noted a connecting wire running down the leg of the table beside him.

"I rather thought the drawer would distract you," he said. "If you try to use that firearm, you'll kill every man in this room. I have but to press on this button and I release a charge of electricity from a wet cell battery, which will explode enough dynamite hidden under the floorboards to blow us to pieces. Gentlemen, I have lived lavishly, but always one step from exposure. The excitement, the zest of having dishonor and disgrace at my elbow constantly, lent a certain vitality and vigor to my aging bones, much as the frost of winter lends strength to the sap of trees and flavor to the fruit they produce. But I had to be prepared for the inevitable, since I figured to face it eventually; and I was determined to go out with as much color and éclat as I could."

"I don't believe you are prepared to destroy yourself," said Holmes in a calm voice.

"While there is the slightest chance, one does not embrace that idea," admitted the exposed tycoon. "But I can use my device to buy time. It's my standard procedure."

His eyes speared me. "Drop that revolver, or you'll have the lives of all around you on your conscience, to say nothing of losing your own."

Since Holmes nodded, I slowly laid my Smith-Webley on the oak table.

Chasseur chuckled. "It's probably an impossible

thing, but I'm going to herd you gentlemen to the far end of the room. I'll be able to reach the door and secure it behind me before you can take action. Perhaps you'll track me down. The odds favor it. But at least I'll have a running start."

I had to admit that Chasseur held us in checkmate. I was horrified when Holmes began to rise from his seat on the bench. His movement drew Chasseur's eye, and the financial charlatan raised the button device in his hand, as though prepared to end it for us all. In that moment, when Chasseur's eyes were glued to the great detective, the man no one was considering moved. My revolver was useless, but there was a walking weapon present who had the uncanny ability to fade into whatever background he found himself. Wakefield Orloff had positioned himself quietly against the wall of the room and had remained there, silent and unmoving, throughout the revelation and drama that followed it. Now his right hand went to the back of his neck and then came forward and down. There was a thud and that wicked Spanish throwing knife that invariably rested in a chamois sheath between his shoulder blades was buried in the leg of the table beside Chasseur. The Tycoon's finger stabbed at the button in his hand and my heart seemed in my throat; but there was no blast of explosives—no carnage, destruction, or death. Orloff's knife had severed the wire neatly, and Chasseur's dynamite trap had been defused.

I swept up my gun, but already Orloff was beside Chasseur, affixing manacles to his wrists. There was a universal sigh of relief from those present to which I contributed.

Chapter 21

❧

Aftermath

TWO MONTHS had passed since the conclusion of what I titled "The Adventure of the Treasure Train." A bright morning sun had dispelled the fog of the previous night and was streaming into our sitting room. Breakfast had come and gone. I was collecting my notes on the schemes of Alvidon Chasseur, with the thought of recording the matter for posterity. Holmes, as was his custom, was perusing the morning papers.

"Here now, Watson," he said suddenly. "We are mentioned by the press and in connection with a strange matter indeed."

I abandoned my work, intrigued of course, and somewhat surprised that Holmes was not regarding me with twinkling eyes, for he viewed newspaper accounts of his exploits with a humorous attitude. Instead, there was a faraway look in his eyes as he folded the journal in half to facilitate reading it to me.

MYSTERIOUS MURDER IN HOLLAND

In Liege but yesterday a resident of the city was felled by what the citizenry are referring to as "the bullet from the sky." Near the town square, Sydney Kokanour, said to be a traveling salesman, was killed instantly by a bullet in his heart. He had lived quietly in Liege since 1891 and was not known to have enemies. Though baffled, the local police have approached the case with the expertise of England's own Sherlock Holmes. The bullet still being in the body, they have established, through the new science of ballistics, that it was fired from a Sharps rifle, a weapon manufactured in America. No one with a rifle was seen anywhere near the vicinity; and there is considerable feeling that the gun might have been fired by mistake, with the bullet, almost spent, unfortunately claiming a victim. Chief Inspector Pyrott of the Liege Police does not concur with this, citing the notorious range of the Sharps Company product. He is of the opinion that some enemy of Kokanour from overseas is behind the matter. An extensive search for such a man is under way.

Holmes lowered the paper, and there was a long silence between us.

"Inspector Pyrott might well be right," he said.

"Indeed, for we have heard mention of the Sharps rifle and in this very room."

"Kokanour took up residence in Liege in 1891."

"The very year you smashed Moriarty. You think Kokanour was Lightfoot McTigue, don't you, Holmes?"

"The thought has crossed my mind."

"But our American friend would have had to know of the assassin."

"He might have caught wind of him while working for Chasseur."

"You feel, then, that he tracked him down?"

"I am considering the possibility that someone was grateful that his considerable past was not exposed; and with that fierce sense of loyalty, not uncommon with those of the frontier, he tried to repay his debt the only way he knew how."

I chewed on this idea for a while. Holmes had risen and was gazing out our bow window. Finally, he turned to me.

"You know, Watson, I've been rather waiting for you to bring the matter up. Now, considering this news, which just may impart a meaning only you and I can understand, I cannot hold my curiosity in check any longer."

"Relative to what?" I queried, but I knew. He had heard me on that momentous afternoon in Essex. Well, it had been enjoyable to cherish my own little secret for a while.

"Our imposter friend. The pseudo-Ledger."

"You disagree with his story of how he came upon the scene?"

"No. That holds water. The idea of a wanted American desperado assuming the identity of a fallen friend and matriculating to Africa and then England is plausible."

"What, then? We could hardly ask the chap to tell us the whole story. After all, he saved our lives."

"Agreed," said Holmes. "But you referred to him by name—McCarty—and he did not deny it."

"There's a story that goes with it," I said, savoring the words.

"I'd like to hear it."

"It begins with the Lincoln County cattle war."

"You mentioned that during our investigation of Trelawney's death in Shaw."

"So I did. Both sides of that bloody frontier incident hired fast guns, and they flocked to New Mexico from everywhere."

"Including the true Ledger," interrupted Holmes in an impatient manner. "I understand all that."

"The Lincoln County war ended in eighteen seventy-eight, with the near total extermination of one side. A survivor was William Bonney, better known as Billy the Kid. The area was under martial law, and General Lew Wallace offered Bonney amnesty."

"Wallace? The same chap who wrote *Ben Hur*?"

"Correct. Bonney refused the general's offer, pointing out that if he hung up his guns, he would not live to see the next sunrise. Later, in eighteen eighty, he was captured by Sheriff Pat Garrett but escaped from jail. Garrett trailed him and shot him in eighteen eighty-one."

"You are indeed a fund of information, Watson; and I recall your mentioning this Billy the Kid previously. But what has this to do with our adventure?"

"There are a couple of holes in the story. For one thing, Bonney was supposedly killed in Fort Sumner, New Mexico, where he was very well liked. For another, Sheriff Pat Garrett was a friend of his."

"Ah-hah!" said Holmes. "You feel all was not as it seemed."

"Rather sure of it. You see, Bonney's real name was Henry McCarty."

The jaw of my friend Sherlock Holmes actually dropped in astonishment. It was a glorious moment, which I shall always cherish.

FOUR FROM
GERALD PETIEVICH

**"Gerald Petievich is...
a fine writer...his dialogue
is pure entertainment."**
**—Elmore Leonard,
Author of *Stick***

☐ 42301-2 To Live And Die In L.A. $3.50

☐ 42224-5 To Die In Beverly Hills $3.50

☐ 41154-5 Money Men $2.50

☐ 41155-3 One-Shot Deal $2.50

Buy them at your local bookstore or use this handy coupon
Clip and mail this page with your order

PINNACLE BOOKS, INC.
Post Office Box 690
Rockville Centre, NY 11571

Please send me the book(s) I have checked above. I am enclosing $_____(please add $1 to cover postage and handling). Send check or money order only—no cash or C.O.D.'s.

Mr./Mrs./Miss_____

Address_____

City_____ State/Zip_____

Please allow six weeks for delivery. Prices subject to change without notice.

LAUGH ALONG WITH
Larry Wilde

"America's bestselling humorist."
—The New York Times

- ☐ 42120-6 THE COMPLETE BOOK OF ETHNIC HUMOR $2.95

- ☐ 41970-8 THE LAST OFFICIAL ITALIAN JOKE BOOK $2.25

- ☐ 41423-4 MORE THE OFFICIAL JEWISH/IRISH JOKE BOOK $1.95

- ☐ 41910-4 MORE THE OFFICIAL SMART KIDS/DUMB PARENTS
  JOKE BOOK $2.25

- ☐ 42004-8 THE NEW OFFICIAL CAT LOVERS JOKE BOOK $1.95

- ☐ 42052-8 THE OFFICIAL BLACK FOLKS/WHITE FOLKS
  JOKE BOOK $2.25

- ☐ 41972-4 THE OFFICIAL BOOK OF SICK JOKES $2.25

- ☐ 41582-6 THE OFFICIAL JEWISH/IRISH JOKE BOOK $2.25

Buy them at your local bookstore or use this handy coupon
Clip and mail this page with your order

PINNACLE BOOKS, INC.
Post Office Box 690
Rockville Centre, NY 11571

Please send me the book(s) I have checked above. I am enclosing $_____(please add $1 to cover postage and handling). Send check or money order only—no cash or C.O.D.'s

Mr./Mrs./Miss_____

Address_____

City_____ State Zip_____

Please allow six weeks for delivery. Prices subject to change without notice

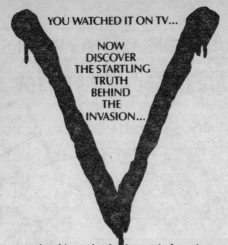

YOU WATCHED IT ON TV...

NOW
DISCOVER
THE STARTLING
TRUTH
BEHIND
THE
INVASION...

...as the ultimate battle for survival continues...

V
by A.C. Crispin
☐ 42237-7/$2.95 ☐ 43231-3/$3.50 (in Canada)
V: EAST COAST CRISIS
by Howard Weinstein and A.C. Crispin
☐ 42259-8/$2.95 ☐ 43251-8/$3.50 (in Canada)
V: THE PURSUIT OF DIANA
by Allen Wold
☐ 42401-9/$2.95 ☐ 43397-2/$3.50 (in Canada)
V: THE CHICAGO CONVERSION
by Geo. W. Proctor
☐ 42429-9/$2.95 ☐ 43417-0/$3.50 (in Canada)
V: THE FLORIDA PROJECT
by Tim Sullivan
☐ 42430-2/$2.95 ☐ 43418-9/$3.50 (in Canada)
V: PRISONERS AND PAWNS
by Howard Weinstein
☐ 42439-6/$2.95 ☐ 43420-0/$3.50 (in Canada)

Buy them at your local bookstore or use this handy coupon
Clip and mail this page with your order

 PINNACLE BOOKS, INC.
Post Office Box 690
Rockville Centre, NY 11571

Please send me the book(s) I have checked above. I am enclosing $_____(please add $1 to cover postage and handling). Send check or money order only—no cash or C.O.D.'s.

Mr./Mrs./Miss_____

Address_____

City_____State/Zip_____

Please allow six weeks for delivery. Prices subject to change without notice.